The Old Tile House

Daphne Neville

Copyright © 2017 Daphne Neville

All rights reserved, including the right to reproduce this book, or portions thereof in any form. No part of this text may be reproduced, transmitted, downloaded, decompiled, reverse engineered, or stored, in any form or introduced into any information storage and retrieval system, in any form or by any means, whether electronic or mechanical without the express written permission of the author.

This is a work of fiction. Names and characters are the product of the author's imagination and any resemblance to actual persons, living or dead, is entirely coincidental.

The views expressed in this work are solely those of the author and do not necessarily reflect the views of the publisher, and the publisher hereby disclaims any responsibility for them.

ISBN: 978-1-326-96183-1

PublishNation, London
www.publishnation.co.uk

Other Titles by this Author

The Ringing Bells Inn
Polquillick
Sea, Sun, Cads and Scallywags
Grave Allegations
The Old Vicarage
A Celestial Affair
Trengillion's Jubilee Jamboree

Chapter One

2013

The waxing moon, almost full, beamed down on the dark sands as the evening train from London Paddington slowly rattled along the track just minutes from its destination. The passengers on the train looked from the opened windows and watched as the waves of the ebbing tide tumbled and splashed onto the deserted, rippled sand before trickling back into the calm darkness of the waters beyond.

As the train slowed, Anna raised her head, put her Kindle back inside her bag and brushed cake crumbs from her lap. She then rose and reached to the rack above for her luggage. The train stopped and after checking that she had all her belongings, Anna walked towards the carriage door and stepped out onto the platform of Penzance station.

Glancing back and forth amongst the already alighted passengers, Anna's eyes eagerly searched through the small crowd, hoping for a glimpse of the tall stranger, who during the latter part of the journey had smiled at her when she had gone to and returned from the buffet car. She felt a pang of disappointment; there was no sign of him. Perhaps he had left the train at St Erth?

Wheeling her suitcase, Anna walked along the platform and outside to the car park, stopping momentarily to take in a breath of the fresh sea air. Parked outside were a few taxis and as she approached the first one, the driver stepped out to greet her.

"Did you have a good journey?" he cheerfully asked, as he opened the back door of the car for Anna.

"Yes, thank you, it was really nice, especially when the train ran alongside the sea in Devon."

"Ah, yes, the scenery there takes a bit of beating." He closed the door, then climbed into the driver's seat and fastened his seatbelt. "Right, miss, where to?"

"The Old Tile House," said Anna, "it's a guest house."

"Oh, yes, I know it," said the driver, reaching for the ignition key. "Lovely old brick built place at the top of the town with three tall chimneys. You don't see much brick in Cornwall because most of the older places are built of granite." He started up the engine and pulled away from the station.

"Is that right?" said Anna, "I must admit it was the picture with its three big chimneys that sold it to me. I thought the description and details sounded interesting too so I hope I'm not disappointed."

"No, I shouldn't think you will be." He chuckled. "And I daresay The Old Tile House like most old places, could tell a tale or two if it were able."

"Yes, I bet they could. So, have you any idea what the owners of the old place I'm going to are like?" Anna asked.

"Very nice from what I've heard although they've not been there long so I've never actually met them. I've picked up several people from the house though and dropped them off as well and I've never heard any complaints."

Anna watched in the semi-darkness from the back window of the taxi as it drove up through the town and then away into residential streets. Eventually, in a quiet tree lined avenue the taxi slowed down and then stopped in front of open wrought iron gates.

"Here we are, miss. This is The Old Tile House although you can't see the house from here because of the trees."

Anna paid the driver as she left the vehicle and he handed her her luggage. She also gave him a generous tip.

"Thank you, miss. I hope you enjoy your stay."

"That's very kind, I'm sure I will."

As the taxi drove away, Anna walked between the open gates and then ambled along the winding driveway pulling her suitcase over the loose gravel. To light up her way in the evolving darkness, four miniature replica street lamps stood amongst the dense shrubbery on either side of the driveway beneath trees that almost touched to form an arch. Fuchsias dripped with red and purple flowers, and hydrangeas bloomed in shades of pink, white and blue. Anna stopped beneath sycamore trees, holly and various firs to look at the hydrangeas. She had never seen any with blue flowers before but knew that the colour was affected by soil pH.

As she touched the large mophead flowers, their colour accentuated in the artificial light, she heard the sound of footsteps on the gravel. Expecting to see someone approaching she turned and looked back along the driveway but to her surprise there was no-one there. Confused, she looked towards the top of the drive but again no-one was visible. Assuming she must have imagined it, she reached for the handle of her suitcase and continued on towards the house.

At the end of the drive Anna found that she was at the back of the building. She paused and looked up to where the three tall imposing chimneys towered high above the rooftop. On the wall in front of her hung a plaque which said 'reception'. Beside it an arrow pointed to her right. Anna followed the arrow round to the front of the house and there stopped and looked out across the gardens which even in the fading light looked impressive. Extensive lawns edged and interspersed with abundant flower beds stretched away to the distant boundary hedge. A hexagonal wooden summerhouse and the silhouette of a large weeping willow tree stood side-by-side and together overlooked the sparkling waters of a moonlit pond.

Thrilled by the house and its location, Anna climbed up five steps, edged by low brick walls and rang the doorbell. A black Labrador ran out barking as the door opened, tail wagging, his curiosity no doubt raised by the arrival of yet another stranger.

"Hello, dear, you must be Annabelle," said the middle-aged lady who had answered the door.

Anna nodded. "Yes, that's me, but please do call me Anna."

"Of course and I'm Michelle, Michelle Templeton," said the lady, as she reached down to take hold of the dog's collar, "and this young rascal is Rafe." She tutted, "I'm afraid he's very boisterous, dear. I do hope you're not afraid of dogs."

Anna leaned forwards and stroked the silky coat and petted the floppy ears. "No, I'm not. How old is he?"

"Fourteen months. We've had him just over a year now and he certainly keeps us on our toes. Anyway, come along inside, Anna, and we'll get you settled."

Anna spoke to Rafe as she stepped over the threshold, "You and I might well be good company for each other because I've always craved a dog like you, but my mum said London was not a suitable place to have one and I suppose to be fair, she was right."

Rafe tilted his head to one side as if to acknowledge her comment; he then ran off down a long corridor and disappeared from view.

Anna put down her suitcase on the black and white tiled floor and looked through her handbag for her purse. "Shall I pay the balance of my fee now?"

"It's up to you, dear. Now or when you leave, we're happy with either."

"In that case I'd like to pay now," said Anna, "so that I can keep an eye on my bank balance." She pulled a debit card from her purse.

"Okay," said Michelle, "come with me."

Anna followed Michelle down the hallway and into a small room which was obviously used as an office.

"Please excuse the mess," said Michelle, tutting as she moved sheets of paper away from the computer, "my husband is a keen genealogist and he clearly hasn't tidied up after his latest bout of delving into the past."

Around all four walls hung pictures of people; some in groups, others alone, some in colour, many in black and white and a few were sepia coloured.

"Are all these people your ancestors?" Anna asked, in awe.

"Yes. James, my husband, is tracking down both our families, bless him. It's become quite an obsession with him, although he hasn't done quite as much since we moved down here simply because both our families lived in various places up-country over the decades. Which of course means the Cornwall Record Office doesn't hold any relevant records for us. It's surprising how much is available on-line though."

After the payment was made, Michelle took Anna upstairs to see her room, situated on the right-hand-side of a wide carpeted landing. Anna glanced around as Michelle unlocked the door. At the end of the landing was a window part-hidden behind white voile curtains. Two other doors were close by, one next to Anna's room and the other directly opposite. To the left of the landing beside the opposite door, ran a narrow passage which led to other rooms.

"As you can see, we've put you in the twin room," said Michelle, as they stepped inside and she switched on the light, "so you have a choice of beds. Please feel free to make use of them both."

Anna looked puzzled. "Oh, but I only paid for a single."

"I know, but we had someone turn up in need of a room a couple of days ago and so I put him in our only single. Don't look alarmed, Anna, it hasn't cost you a penny more."

"Thank you, lucky me," Anna said, glancing around the L shaped room, "it's beautiful and so spacious. And I have two windows as well as two beds."

"Yes," said Michelle, pulling the curtains across each in turn. "The big one with the window seat looks to the south; the smaller one faces east and so you'll get the early morning sun in there."

"Perfect. I feel I'm being spoilt."

Michelle laughed. "We also have a lounge downstairs for our guests, so please feel free to make use of it. I ought to have pointed it out just now but it's easy enough to find. It's at the bottom of the stairs and the only door on the left."

Anna nodded to show her gratitude. "Thank you, I shall probably do that this evening once I've settled in."

As Michelle left the room, Anna took from her voluminous handbag a rather old teddy bear and sat him down on the pillow of her chosen bed for the first night.

"Well, Andy, we're here and I don't know about you but I get a lovely feeling about this place." She stroked his head. "What's more, I think this is going to be the best holiday ever."

After she had unpacked her suitcase and hung her clothes in the large built-in wardrobe which took up the entire length of space behind the door, Anna made herself a cup of coffee and ate one of the complimentary ginger biscuits she had found in a cellophane bag on the tea tray, she then took a shower. Afterwards, having made up her mind that she did not want to watch television alone in her room, she decided to go down to the lounge and take her Kindle to read just in case no-one else was in there.

On the landing, as she closed her door, she noticed a key was in the lock of the room next to hers and wondered if perhaps someone had forgotten to take it with them. She made a mental note to mention it if she met anyone downstairs.

A jingling noise caused her to pause at the foot of the stairs. On looking up she saw that a mini chandelier dangled from the ceiling by the front door. She watched, mesmerised, as it swayed in the draught from an open window and cast flickering shadows on the surrounding walls.

Inside the guests' lounge, a couple in their sixties were sitting at a table, playing cards. They looked up as Anna peeped around the door.

"Come in, come in," said the male, beckoning her inside, "I take it you're the young lady who Michelle told us was due to join us here today."

"Yes," said Anna, surprised, "I arrived a couple of hours ago."

As she entered the room and closed the door, the man rose from his seat at the table and held out his hand. "I'm Brian Cooke and this is my good wife, Brenda. We're otherwise known as BBC," he chuckled.

"Lovely to meet you. My name is Anna Greenwood," she said shaking the proffered hand.

Brenda rose and gave her a hug. "And it's very nice to meet you too, Anna."

"Now," said Brian, as he sat back down, gathering up the cards on the table and shuffling them, "would you like to join us for a game or two?"

Anna bit her bottom lip. "It all depends what you're playing. I'm afraid I don't know many card games."

"That's okay, we can play whatever you like," said Brenda, returning to her chair.

"I know how to play rummy although I've not played it for years and so might be a little rusty."

"Rummy it is then and you'll soon get the hang of it again." Brian pulled out a chair for Anna. "Sit down, lass but first pour yourself a glass of wine." He indicated two bottles of merlot on a sideboard beside a tray of glasses.

Anna did as she was instructed and then sat down. "Surely the wine isn't on the house."

Brenda laughed. "No, it's not, dear. But Michelle and James said they had no objection to us enjoying a drink while under their roof and provided us with the glasses."

"We're publicans," said Brian, with a grin, "so having a drink has become a bit of a habit with us."

Anna smiled. "I see."

As Brian dealt out the cards, Anna looked around the spacious room. The table at which they sat was next to a window that was completely hidden behind plush floor length curtains. On one of the long walls was an ornate wooden fireplace, its grate concealed by a solid brass fire screen. To one side of the fireplace stood a leather two-seater settee and opposite it was a matching three-seater. Two of the walls were completely hidden behind dark wooden shelving which ran from floor to ceiling, the only break in one being the space for the door into the hall. On the upper and lower shelves, books ran from end to end. On the middle shelves stood hundreds of Toby jugs in all shapes and sizes.

"What a lot of books," said Anna, craning her neck to see, "and what a lot of Toby jugs."

"Yes," said Brenda, picking up her cards, "according to James, this room used to be the library and when he and Michelle viewed the house the previous owners had the shelves crammed full with books, many of which had come from a secondhand bookshop they'd run once upon a time." She laughed. "But James said when they moved in they didn't have anywhere near enough books even to fill the shelves on one wall let alone two, and so they've utilised the spare space with Michelle's collection of Toby jugs. I think it looks rather effective, don't you?"

Anna agreed, "Yes, I do, and some of their expressions are priceless."

"Quite," said Brenda, "but I don't envy Michelle the task of dusting them all."

"It's quiet in here tonight," said Brian, scowling at the cards in his hand, "I can even hear the old clock ticking."

"Are we the only guests? Anna asked.

Brian nodded. "Yes, at the moment it's just us three and the vicar."

Anna pulled a face. "Vicar, I must be on my best behaviour then."

"I don't think you'll need to do that," said Brian, with a chuckle, "this chap seems a bit of a trendy. You know, dresses like other young lads and so forth and always looking at his phone."

"He doesn't say much either," said Brenda, "so I think he's rather boring."

Anna giggled. "I see."

"Of course, there were more people here but they all went home this morning," said Brian, "but I daresay there will be more arrivals during the coming week."

"Oh, there will be," said Brenda, with enthusiasm, "and it'll be lovely when they do arrive. We've only been here a couple of days ourselves you see, Anna, and so we didn't have time to get to know the folks that went home this morning which is a shame because some of them seemed really nice."

Brian tutted. "As you can see, Anna, my wife is an extrovert. Put her in a room full of people and she's as happy as Larry."

Anna laughed. "My mum used to use that saying but I never did get round to asking her who Larry was."

"Well, there are two possible answers," said Brian, "and both come from down under. He was either an Australian boxer called Larry Foley who never lost a fight and when he retired at the age of thirty two got a thousand pounds for his last match, which was a lot of money back in the eighteen seventies."

"And so he'd have been very happy," said Brenda, didactically.

"Quite," said Brian, "and the other possibility derives from what was originally a Cornish word which later became used in Australia and New Zealand: the word being larrikin - a slang term meaning a rough chap or hooligan who larks about and who was undoubtedly happy."

"Brilliant," said Anna, "I think I like the second theory best as we're in Cornwall."

Brenda nodded. "I'm inclined to agree, dear, as I'm none too fond of boxing."

A little later as the clock on the mantelpiece struck eleven, Anna, who had by then consumed several glasses of red wine, confessed to feeling sleepy. She rose unsteadily to her feet.

"I'm sure you'll not be offended if I deprive you of my company," she giggled, "it's been a very long day. In fact it seems forever ago that I got up."

"Of course not," said Brenda, gathering the cards and returning them to the pack, "we ought to be making a move too."

"Oh, I've just remembered. There's a key in the lock of the room next to mine. Do you think someone forgot to take it out with them? Having said that, if the only guests are you, me and the vicar then it might not be the case."

"I think you'll find that room will be unoccupied," said Brenda, "and Michelle leaves the keys in the locks so that they don't get lost."

Brian nodded. "Yes, our key was certainly in the lock when we arrived because I remember seeing it before Michelle took us in there."

Anna tutted. "Now you come to mention it the key was already in my door too. Silly me." She turned to leave. "Goodnight."

"Yes, goodnight, dear. See you at breakfast."

"Oh, yes, breakfast. What time is it?" Anna asked. "I can't remember whether or not Michelle told me."

Brenda nodded. "It's between eight and nine-thirty, but Michelle says they're very forgiving if guests are a little late."

Anna smiled. "I shall make sure I'm on time. I don't want to create a bad impression on my first morning."

Anna climbed the wide staircase and then walked along the carpeted landing to her bedroom door. Once inside her room, she undressed and put on her long nightdress, removed her make-up and cleaned her teeth.

Before she climbed into bed, she switched off the light and pulled back both sets of curtains, for Anna preferred to sleep with the curtains undrawn. Attracted towards the lights of the town, she knelt down on the window seat of the south facing window and then looked up to the night sky. The near-full moon stood out brightly amongst the twinkling stars and the silhouette of St Michael's Mount stood out on the horizon.

Feeling happy and sleepy, she then pulled back the duvet and plumped up the white pillows. As she snuggled down beneath the sweet smelling bed linen with her old teddy bear, she sighed, much contented.

"Goodnight, Andy. Sleep tight, my love."

Chapter Two

On Sunday morning, Anna woke to see the sun streaming in through the small window in her room, causing a crystal vase on its wooden sill to sparkle and cast coloured flecks of light onto the patterned beige carpet.

"Yippee," she said, stretching her arms, "it's September the first and my favourite month."

Eager to see Penzance in daylight, she slid from her bed and crossed to the cushioned seat of the south facing window where she knelt and gazed down onto the sumptuous gardens below. Enthralled, she looked across the impeccable lawns and the immaculate flower beds to the roof tops of Penzance and the outline of the coast on the horizon. She had read on The Old Tile House website that the proprietors were dedicated gardeners but had not expected to witness such perfection or to have been allocated a room with so wonderful a view.

"It's like looking onto a park," giggled Anna, as she dashed into the bathroom for a quick shower, eager to get outside and feel the warmth of the early September sunshine on her face. However, as she closed the bathroom door, she remembered her dream; the man from the train, she had dreamed of him. She sighed, and wistfully wondered where he might be.

There were no new guests in the morning room when Anna went in for breakfast but Michelle was there; she greeted her warmly and said to sit wherever she liked. From a table by the window, Brenda and Brian Cooke waved as she took a seat near to the fireplace where an array of colourful dried flowers concealed the blackened grate. To Anna's amazement she saw that Brian and Brenda were drinking champagne.

"It's our Ruby Wedding Anniversary today," said Brenda, amused by the surprised look on Anna's face. "Would you like a glass of bubbly?"

"That's very kind, but no thank you. I don't think I could face it this early in the day."

Brian chuckled. "We're finding it's slipping down very well."

By the door sat a young man with thick, dark hair wearing a striped rugby shirt and jeans. As he rose to leave the room, Anna was surprised to see that he wore a dog collar and therefore must be the vicar of whom Brian and Brenda had spoken the previous evening.

After breakfast, Anna went outside to the gardens to explore. She peeked into the summerhouse, then sat down beneath a laden Bramley apple tree on a bench that wrapped around the entire girth of the knotted trunk.

With her eyes closed she listened to bird song and the tuneful whistle which emanated from the nearby vegetable plot. The *click* of a closing gate caused her to open her eyes whereupon she saw a cheeky faced man, clad in a grey shirt, faded jeans and gumboots. In his hand he held a pair of secateurs and beside him was Rafe.

"Ah, you must be Annabelle," said the stranger, looking her up and down.

Anna sat up and straightened her back. "Yes, yes I'm Annabelle but how on earth did you know that?"

"You might say I heard it on the grapevine. The Old Tile House is a very friendly guest house. Home from home so to speak."

"Hmm, so it said on the website. But as regards my name, if you call me Annabelle I might not answer as everyone I know calls me Anna and always have done."

"Anna it is then."

"And may I ask who you are?"

"I'm Alfie, Alfie Trewin and I do the gardening here."

"So I see," smiled Anna, as she stood and held out her hand, "it's nice to meet you, Alfie. And I have to say you're doing a splendid job, the gardens are quite magnificent, especially the roses."

He shook her hand. "Thank you for the compliments, I do my best but I can't take all the credit because James does his fair share."

"James?" queried Anna.

"My boss," said Alfie.

"Oh, I see, yes, of course. Michelle did mention her husband was called James but I've not met him yet."

"You'll like him, he's a really nice bloke. Anyway, I'd better get on."

Anna smiled. "Yes, of course."

Resuming his whistling, Alfie walked over to a flower bed where he proceeded to snip off the faded flowers of the summer bedding. Rafe, however, chose to sit by Anna's side where she stroked his coat and tickled him under his jaw.

A sudden noise caused Anna to look towards the house where an upstairs window had crashed open. A young woman looked out and shouted, "Morning, Alfie."

Alfie looked up and waved the secateurs. "Time you were up, lazybones."

The person at the window pulled an unladylike face and then disappeared from view.

"Who is that?" Anna asked, "I don't think she can be one of the guests otherwise Brenda and Brian would have mentioned her."

Alfie grinned. "She's not a guest, she's Poppy, the boss's daughter. She's home from university and is supposed to help out in the bed and breakfast but she's seldom up in time for breakfast."

Anna laughed. "I see. Well I know very little about students other than the fact that they're not renowned for being early risers."

"Yes, that's Poppy alright, although to be fair she does take care of the rooms most days but Michelle and James wouldn't mind if she did nothing; they're just glad to have her home."

"Is she their only child then?"

Alfie nodded. "Yep."

Anna was still sitting beneath the apple tree stroking Rafe when Poppy emerged from the house holding a slice of buttered toast. Hoping she might have something for him, Rafe ran to greet her and then to Anna's surprise Poppy sat down beside her.

"Hi, I've come to introduce myself. I'm Poppy and it's great to see we have a guest staying here who doesn't qualify for a free bus pass."

Anna laughed. "Most of the guests who come here are elderly then?"

"Ninety nine point nine percent, yes," said Poppy.

Alfie tutted. "Just as well you're not studying maths, Pops, or you'd fail dismally."

Poppy sighed. "Okay then, perhaps it's nowhere near ninety nine point nine percent, but most are couples anyway so there's never anyone I can latch on to."

"I spotted a vicar during breakfast this morning who was both young, handsome and alone," Anna teased. "He also looked quite trendy."

"Yes, but he's a vicar so hardly likely to be a barrel of laughs."

Anna shook her head. "You may well be wrong there. I knew a vicar once who was both amusing and good company."

Poppy raised her eyebrows.

"And so was his wife," Anna added.

Poppy laughed.

"Anyway, why would you need to find a friendly soul amongst the guests?" Anna continued, "I mean, surely you have friends of your own."

"At uni, yes, but not here in Penzance. We used to live in Wiltshire, you see, and Mum and Dad bought this place just after I started at uni so I've never really had a chance to get to know any of the locals as I'm only home during the holidays."

"You've got me," said Alfie, with a grin.

"Yeah, I got you, flappy ears, but it's nice to have female company too."

Alfie's eyebrows rose. "Perhaps Anna won't want your company."

"Oh, I will," said Anna, with enthusiasm, "really, it'll be nice to have someone to talk to."

Alfie, having finished the dead-heading left the girls chatting and walked over to the greenhouse.

"So have you made any plans for today?" Poppy asked.

Anna shook her head. "No, nothing apart from coming out here to see the garden."

"Fancy a dip in the old briny later then? I like to go as often as possible but get bored going on my own."

Poppy didn't look overly-keen. "Actually, I can't swim."

"Well, when I say a dip, I mean a paddle. I seldom go into the sea because it's too cold."

Anna laughed. "In that case, count me in."

"Brilliant. I have to do the rooms first but it won't take long as only three are occupied, and you only arrived yesterday so I assume you've not made a mess yet."

Anna giggled. "I think you'll find that I've not made a mess at all."

"Excellent. That means I only have to make your bed and wipe round in the bathroom. It doesn't take long to do the Cookes' room either because Brenda always makes the bed, bless her. The vicar's a bit messy though. Anyway, I should be finished in an hour so I'll meet you here at eleven."

"I'll be ready. Meanwhile I shall take another wander around the garden and smell the roses again. I see you have some yellow ones over there and I'm very fond of yellow roses."

Anna strolled down towards the pond with Rafe by her side, she then walked over to the summer house and sat on the steps of its veranda. With her elbows rested on her knees, she watched a black cat washing as it sat on a shed roof just visible over the top of a hedge which bordered the next door garden. Rafe watched too but made no attempt to bark at his feline neighbour.

Over by the shrubs which ran alongside the driveway, a wheelbarrow stood laden with trimmings from the various bushes and trees. Leaning on its side was a pair of long-handled shears.

At the top of the garden beyond the house and on the edge of the fenced off vegetable plot, Alfie was in the greenhouse picking tomatoes. Anna watched him but turned her head when, from the driveway behind the shrubs, she heard the sound of footsteps crunching across the gravel. No-one was visible but then as the footsteps reached the top of the driveway, the vicar appeared and walked onto the path with a newspaper clutched in his hand. Without looking around, he hurriedly went into the house by way of the front door.

A sudden splash in the pond caused Anna to look towards the water. She was too late to see its source but observed a lily pad quivering in the rippling water and so assumed its disturbance might have been caused by the swift movement of a fish or a frog.

Disappointed, she looked back towards the driveway and saw that the wheelbarrow laden with trimmings had moved. Thinking Alfie must be close by she glanced around to see where he was. To her surprise he was still inside the greenhouse. Anna glanced back at the wheelbarrow only to see that it had moved yet again and the shears were lying on the grass. She stood up and crossed to where the barrow stood. There was no-one close by, or even in the garden, other than herself, Alfie and Rafe.

Anna and Poppy met as planned and once on the beach they removed their shoes.

"So if it's not being too nosy, may I ask what brings you to Cornwall in September and all on your own?" Poppy asked as they slowly ambled across the dry sand, pleasantly warmed by the sun.

"Of course I don't mind telling you," said Anna. "It's quite straight forward really. I chose September simply because I assumed it would be a lot quieter than during the summer when the schools are on holiday, I know they still are on holiday but only for a few more days. And I'm on my own because I wanted to be free to come and go as I please. My mother grew up in Devon, you see, and we had one or two holidays there, but for some reason I always wanted to come further down and visit Cornwall, especially Penzance. But Mum always said there was no point because Devon was just as lovely as Cornwall and I suppose to be fair, it is."

"Yes, I daresay, so why were you keen to come to Penzance?"

Anna give a little laugh. "I don't really know but can only assume it was because when I was young Mum took me to see *The Pirates of Penzance*. I loved the name and dreamed that one day I'd come here."

"And now you have."

"Yes, my only regret is that I wasn't able to bring Mum with me."

Poppy smiled. "Don't tell me, she wouldn't come because she still thinks Devon is best?"

Anna shook her head. "Sadly that's not the reason. Well, yes, she probably would still say that were she alive but regrettably she died nearly four years ago just before Christmas."

"Oh, I am sorry, Anna. That's really sad. She couldn't have been very old."

Anna sighed. "No, she was just forty."

"Similar age to my mum," said Poppy, thoughtfully.

"Yes."

"So, do you have any brothers or sisters?"

Anna shook her head. "No, I have no family and so am all alone in the world apart from a few friends, that is."

Poppy gulped. "What, no family at all?"

"No-one."

Poppy frowned. "But surely you must have some aunts, uncles, grandparents and a few cousins perhaps?"

"I've no-one, at least no-one I know of. In reality I suppose I must have relatives somewhere but I don't know of them and they don't know of me."

Poppy looked confused.

"My mother was adopted, you see, when she was just six weeks old following the death of her parents in a car crash. That's how she ended up in Devon; her adoptive parents lived there."

"Oh, I see. That sort of makes sense now." Poppy paused to pick up a crisp packet discarded on the sand. "So, do you know whereabouts in Devon she used to live? I only ask because I have a friend at uni who lives there."

"In a village just outside Exeter. I can't remember its name because it's years since we last went there."

"Hmm, anyway at least that explains your mother's affection for Devon."

"Yes, she lived there throughout her childhood and then when she was fifteen she and her adoptive parents went to live somewhere or other in the Taunton area because of a job promotion for her adoptive father or something like that."

"Ah, I see. So were you born in Somerset?"

"No, I was born in Battersea." Anna laughed at the confused look on Poppy's face. "You see, when Mum was twenty she left her Taunton home and went to London to seek her fortune. She had a good voice and hoped to make a career for herself as a singer. Sadly, her musical dreams never came to fruition and she spent most of her time working in bars and restaurants." Anna sighed. "I never knew my father but because Mum worked as a waitress I've always assumed that he was probably a chef. Mum never spoke of him and was happy to bring me up as a single parent. But it was a struggle which eventually took its toll. She died when I was nineteen years old."

"Oh, Anna, that's so sad."

"Yes."

"So, how did your mother manage to work when you were little?"

"She had a friend who also had a child and so they took it in turns to look after us while the other worked or we'd go to nursery school. I don't remember much about it but I was always well cared for."

As they neared a litter bin, Poppy dropped the empty crisp packet inside. "So your father is out there somewhere but you've no idea where."

"I suppose so, but who knows what happened to him. He could be dead for all I know. Whatever though, he doesn't know that I exist simply because Mum never told him."

"I wonder why?"

"I always got the impression that he might have been married and so she broke off their relationship as soon as she found out about me. I like to think she didn't want to come between him and his wife permanently, but that's only a theory and I've no evidence to back it up." She laughed. "Although I do like cooking so if he was a chef I may have inherited my culinary skills from him. On the other hand, maybe that's just me grasping at straws."

"It must be horrible to know nothing of your past," said Poppy, thoughtfully. "Dad's mad about genealogy and has traced his and Mum's families way back to goodness know when."

"Yes, when I arrived your mum had to move some of his research to get to the computer."

Poppy tutted. "Yes, I can imagine. So do you still live in London?"

"Yes, but I had to give up the small furnished flat Mum rented in Battersea after she died simply because I couldn't afford it. I work in a hotel as a receptionist, you see, and so back then our combined wages just about made ends meet."

"So, where do you live now?"

"I moved into another furnished flat with three girls who are my workmates. They needed someone else because a previous flat mate had recently left to live with her boyfriend and without her money they were finding the rent a little steep. The space we have is rather limited, but then it hardly matters as my worldly goods are little more than a few items of clothing and my faithful old teddy bear."

"Would that be the bear I saw on your pillow when I did your room this morning?"

"Yes, his name is Andy and he's my best friend."

"So, don't you have a boyfriend?"

Anna shook her head. "Not now. I did have but we parted company four months ago. He was a French student, you see and so when his course finished he went home. We still keep in touch but as friends now."

"That's nice. So do you speak French?"

"Languages were never my best subjects at school but thankfully Pierre spoke excellent English." Anna laughed. "He tried to help me improve my French but eventually gave up."

"So Andy the bear is your best friend now?"

Anna nodded.

Poppy hung her head. "You know, at times I often think I'm hard done by, Anna, but you've made me realise just how much I have."

"Hmm, at times I have felt sorry for myself, especially since Mum left me and I became all alone in the world, but I remind myself that there are always a lot of people far worse off than me." She gave a sudden nervous laugh. "Anyway, that's more than enough about me. So please, do tell, are you and Alfie an item?"

Poppy shook her head and then laughed. "No, and to use that old banal phrase, we're just good friends."

"Oh, but I got the impression he was rather smitten with you."

Poppy smiled. "I don't think so. He knows I have a boyfriend at uni, although to be honest it's nothing serious and Alfie is aware of that."

"So, what's the story behind Alfie? I mean, does he just garden for your parents or does he do other things as well?"

Poppy stopped walking. "Let's sit down here. I really can't be bothered to go any further."

They sat down on the sand.

Alfie has a troubled past," said Poppy, resting her elbows on her raised knees, "because he has a broken marriage behind him. He used to work for an estate agents and was there for quite a few years. Anyway, to cut a long story short, he married the boss's daughter, but sadly the marriage didn't last because his wife met someone else. Poor Alfie was shattered when he found out. At the time he and his wife were renting a house together while they looked for somewhere suitable to buy. Fortunately they hadn't found anywhere that they both liked and got themselves tied up with a mortgage so Alfie was able to leave their rented house with no obligations when he found out about his wife's new bloke. And after he moved out her new chap moved in. It makes me so cross, I'd like to wring her neck. Alfie's so kind hearted and deserves better than that."

"Poor Alfie," said Anna, "So where did he go? Does he have family nearby?"

"Yes, his parents live in Helston and he has a sister who lives in Pentrillick but rather than bother any of them he moved in with a friend and slept on his sofa. To be honest, I don't think he wanted to face his mother straight away because apparently she never really liked his choice of wife anyway. His sister would have been sympathetic but then he didn't want to bother her because she hadn't been married long herself."

"Oh dear, what a mess."

"Absolutely, but that's not all. He also left the office and gave up his job because he couldn't bear to work with his ex. His ex-father-in-law was absolutely livid. He liked Alfie, you see, and thought he had a great future. I'm told that he was disgusted with his daughter's behaviour and relations between them have been strained ever since. Not that I've ever met any of the party involved, other than Alfie, that is. It's Dad who's gleaned all the details because he and Alfie get on well together."

"That's awful," said Anna. "How long were they married for?"

"Just seven months and thankfully they had no children."

"So how did it come about that he took up gardening?"

"When we moved to The Old Tile House the garden was neglected and badly overgrown and so Dad really needed someone to help him get it back to how it must have been in the past. He and Alfie first met in a pub where Dad was watching some men play pool and Alfie was one of them was. Alfie asked Dad if he'd like a game and it went from there. Dad learned that Alfie did horticulture at school for one of his GCSE subjects and that he really liked it. He lives with us too and has one of the attic rooms which is really nice. Nicer than my room in fact but then I'm not here much."

"The gardens are a credit to him," said Anna, drawing a flower in the sand.

"Yes, they are. He does other things too. You know, decorating and odd jobs. Mum and Dad have frequently said that they don't know what they'd do without him." Poppy suddenly stood up and began to roll up the legs of her jeans. "Come on, Anna, we've done more than enough chatting. It's time we went in for a paddle."

Anna groaned. "I'd hoped you'd forgotten that was the purpose of our coming here."

"You wimp," said Poppy, grabbing Anna's hands and dragging her to her feet.

"Now roll up your jeans and I'll race down to the water."

As anticipated the sea was cold. Anna screamed as the waves splashed up her legs.

"Brrr, it's freezing, this is torture."

"Awe, yes, it is. I don't know how anyone can swim in here without a wetsuit," said Poppy, jumping in and out of the small waves, "I can feel my feet going numb and that's in just a few inches of water."

"I don't think I'd like to wear a wetsuit," said Anna, stepping back onto the warm sand, "they look terribly restrictive and uncomfortable, but as a non-swimmer I wouldn't know."

"Oh, they're fine," said Poppy, also leaving the water, "in fact Alfie and I are going to Newquay on Wednesday, surfing. I have a spare wetsuit so you must come too."

"Surfing," said Anna, a look of horror on her face, "I wouldn't be any good at that. Besides, I can't swim."

"You never know till you've tried and it doesn't matter too much whether or not you can swim when a beginner. Anyway, Alfie has done a course on life saving so you'll be alright."

"I shall feel like a gooseberry," said Anna, drying her cold feet on a towel.

Poppy growled. "I've already told you that there's nothing between Alfie and me. Oh, please, say that you'll come. It'll be fun."

Anna quickly wracked her brains to think up a plausible excuse but to her disgust her mind was blank. "Okay," she said, "but you may well regret it as I'm sure to be an embarrassment to you both."

Chapter Three

Anna woke up on Monday morning feeling full of energy and by eight o'clock was showered and dressed; to help Poppy, she'd even made her bed.

Leaving Andy on the window ledge so that he could enjoy the view over the garden she then went down to breakfast where she was surprised to find that Poppy had also risen early and was in the kitchen helping her mother, Michelle.

"I was wondering," said Poppy, as she cleared away Anna's breakfast dishes, "if you'd like to take a walk along the coastal path to Marazion. With me, of course. We could even go over the causeway to St Michael's Mount if we felt like it. It's a smashing walk which I vow to do quite often but it's not the same going on my own."

"Sounds great," said Anna, "I do like walking and should like to see as much of the area as possible."

"Excellent," said Poppy, "I have to do the rooms first but should have them done in a jiffy. Well, perhaps a bit longer than a jiffy because I need to get one of the unoccupied doubles ready for new guests arriving later today. It shouldn't take long though because the bed is made so it's just a case of making sure all the odds and sods are in place."

"Odds and sods?" Anna queried.

"Yes, you know, ginger biscuits, tea bags and stuff like that."

"Yes, of course, I see."

"I should be done by half eleven so I'll see you then. Any idea where you'll be?"

"Outside," said Anna, without hesitation, "idling somewhere in the garden."

To pass the time while Poppy was doing the rooms, Anna put on a little make-up and changed into shoes suitable for walking; she then went out into the garden and sat down beside the pond. The wheelbarrow which the day before had seemed to have a life of its own was no longer by the shrubs and on looking around it seemed that no-one else was in the garden at all.

Anna laid down on the grass and with her eyes closed drank in the quietness: such a contrast she thought compared with the hustle and bustle of London, for the only sound to be heard in the garden was the hum of cars in the distance and the occasional splash in the pond of a darting fish. However, a sudden noise made her jump and a shrill voice called from next door, "Henry, Henry, oh, there you are. Come along, dear, breakfast's ready."

Anna thought it a little late for breakfast but then perhaps Henry and his wife or whoever she was were not early risers. She stood up and walked over to the boundary hedge and tried to peer through into next door's garden but all she could see were shrubs and more shrubs.

"Looking for birds' nests?" asked a jovial voice from behind.

Anna jumped and turned quickly to see Alfie sprinkling fish food into the pond.

"I was just, um, I…, oh damn, I was being nosy. I heard a woman's voice next door, you see, and was trying to see who it was. Oh, dear, that sounds really bad. You must think me a dreadful busybody."

"No, not really. It must have been Martha you heard. She's knocking on a bit and her hearing's not too good but she's a lively soul." He grinned cheekily. "If you want a better view of her garden then go into the veg plot and stand on top of the compost heap. You get a smashing view from there."

"Stop it," said Anna, lightly punching his arm, "you're making me feel really bad."

"Oy, what are you up to?" asked Poppy as she strode across the lawn. "I hope you're not harassing the guests, Alfie Trewin."

"Just teasing," he said, winking at Anna.

Anna blushed. "Yes, and I hate to admit it, Poppy, but I think Alfie's mockery was entirely justified."

It was nearly midday by the time Anna and Poppy left The Old Tile House and walked down through the town towards the railway and bus stations, beyond which was access to the coastal path.

The path ran twixt the railway tracks and the sea for much of the way, then once past Long Rock it veered off across the beach amongst tussocks of grass and over a stream. Anna was particularly taken with the clusters of sea holly whose once blue, prickly flowers, had long since faded and dried out in the sun and salt air.

"I'm pretty sure we have some of them growing in our garden," said Poppy after Anna had expressed her admiration of the flowers, "although I daresay they'll be a cultivated variety whereas these are no doubt wild."

"Really. So do you have an interest in flowers?"

"Good heavens, no. They're much too mundane for me."

"So how come you know of the sea holly?"

Poppy laughed. "Through Alfie of course. He often twitters on about flowers, herbs and vegetables but to be honest he seldom gets my full attention. The sea holly registered with me though simply because they're different from the ordinary every day showy flowers."

"I see. I take it you're not studying horticulture or botany at uni then."

"Most certainly not, but then no doubt you're just being facetious, aren't you?" She cast a knowing look in Anna's direction and smiled. "I'm actually studying science and I love it."

Anna turned up her nose. "Ugh, that's my worst subject ever. Give me mundane flowers any day."

On arriving back at The Old Tile House, Poppy insisted Anna go with her into the kitchen to make themselves cups of coffee. Anna felt that as a paying guest the kitchen should be out of bounds but Poppy assured her she was also a friend.

In the kitchen they found Michelle, making ginger biscuits for the guest room tea trays on which tea and coffee making provisions were presented.

"Coffee, Mum?" Poppy asked as she reached for the kettle.

"I'd rather have tea, please. I've already had more cups of coffee than I ought."

Poppy filled the kettle. "Sit down, Anna. We'll have our coffee in here."

Anna sat. "Is there anything I can do to help?" she asked Michelle.

"No thanks, love. I've made these so often I reckon I could make them in my sleep."

"You're very clever making them yourself; they're delicious: so much better than those sold in shops."

"Thank you," said Michelle, as she put the last of the biscuits on a tray and popped it into the oven. "I use the same recipe that my mother has used for years." She sat down at the table with Anna to await her tea. "So, have you done anything interesting today?"

"Hmm, yes, we went to St Michael's Mount and it was surprisingly busy for September, but then the weather is nice, I suppose."

"Good, and did you walk or have to go by boat?"

"We walked there and back," said Poppy, placing three mugs on the table, "The tide was right out, you see, and as we didn't stay long we were able to get back on foot too."

"That was lucky. So, what did you think of it, Anna?"

Anna frowned. "I thought it was beautiful and loved being able to look back to the mainland from there. It was really weird though because I felt I'd been there before which is daft because this is my first visit to Cornwall."

"She even knew her way round," said Poppy, slipping off her shoes beneath the table, "which was a bit freaky."

The sound of tyres crunching over the gravel at the back of the house caused Poppy's ears to prick up. "Ah, do you think that might be the new guests arriving?"

Michelle rolled her eyes. "It'll more likely be your father as he went out for some shopping a while back. I doubt it's the new guests anyway as they're already here unless they popped out and I didn't hear them go."

"They're already here? Oh, so what are they like?"

"Hmm, well, I suppose if I'm honest I'd say they are rather strange."

"That sounds a little ominous," said Poppy, her eyebrows raised. "Tell me more. I mean, what's strange about them?"

"Well, I suppose to be fair I shouldn't say strange but *he* is certainly a bit odd. Not sure about *her* because she didn't say very much." Michelle put her mug down on the table. "You're never going to believe this, girls, but apparently he is a ghost hunter. His name is Dominic and his girlfriend is called Josephina but she likes to be called Jo."

"I can't say that I blame her," said Poppy. "What sort of age are they?"

Michelle shrugged her shoulders. "I'd say she's in her thirties and he's in his forties. It's not always possible to tell these days."

Anna smiled. "Neither of them eligible for a bus pass then."

Poppy giggled. "No, not by the sound of it."

"Bus pass," said Michelle, "why would they want a bus pass?"

"Oh, it's nothing, just a silly comment I made the other day." Poppy looked guilty.

"Don't you think it's a bit creepy, this chap Dominic being a ghost hunter, I mean?" Anna asked, hoping to sway the subject away from the derogatory comments Poppy had made regarding the ages of guests.

"Yes, I do," said Michelle. "And there's another thing. When I took them up to their room his eyes were darting all over the place and he was grinning like a Cheshire cat. I thought that was a bit creepy too."

"So is their stay in Cornwall for business or pleasure?" Poppy asked.

"Both," said Michelle, picking up her mug again, "although I can't see there is much to differentiate between the two."

Anna was intrigued as well as apprehensive. "So where on earth will they be ghost hunting? Not this house, I hope."

Michelle laughed. "He'd be wasting his time if he was because I don't think he'd find any ghosts here. But then this isn't his target, because he told me that they are going to spend a night at Pengersick Castle. I've heard that they hold such events as ghost hunts there from time to time."

Anna shuddered. "Well rather them than me."

"Hmm, not sure that I agree," said Poppy. "In fact I've a feeling that Dominic and Josephina might turn out to be the most interesting guests we've ever had stay here."

"Is that wishful thinking, Poppy, or are you suddenly clairvoyant?" Michelle asked as she rose to open the door for James who had bags of shopping.

Poppy rubbed her chin thoughtfully. "Probably a bit of both."

In the evening, Anna and Poppy went out for a drink in Penzance and called in at the first pub that they came across. They sat at a table quite close to the bar but as they chatted Poppy observed that every time the door opened, Anna promptly turned her head.

"Are you expecting someone?" Poppy asked when she could no longer suppress her curiosity.

"What? Oh, no, no." Anna frowned, "of course not. Why do you ask?"

"Because your eyes seem to be fixed on that door. Not once has it opened without you quickly turning to look at it."

Anna bit her bottom lip. "Sorry, I didn't realise I was being that obvious."

"Well, you are. So, who or what are you looking for?" Poppy leaned forward and rested her elbows on the table. "You have to tell me or I shall have no choice other than to make wild and perhaps ludicrous guesses."

Anna giggled. "Actually if I do tell, you'll think me extremely daft."

"Perhaps, but let me be the judge of that."

"Okay, right, well, I'm looking out for a man that I saw on the train when I came down here. I know it's crazy because I don't even know that he's in Penzance and certainly have no reason to believe that he might come in here. It's just, well, I can't get his face out of my mind."

Poppy tilted her head to one side. "Hmm, you're right I do think you're daft, having said that I'd like to hear more. I mean, who was he? What did he look like? Why do you want to see him again?"

Anna shrugged her shoulders. "I've absolutely no idea who he was but without doubt he was handsome and I'd say he was probably in his forties. You see, I didn't really get that good a look at him but he was in the next coach to me and I saw him when I went to the buffet car. He smiled as I passed him and then smiled again when I was on my way back."

"Is that it?"

"Yes, well no. Sometime later after the train left Camborne I popped to the loo and I saw him again through the glass door of the next coach, which means that he had to have got off at either St Erth or here in Penzance because the train didn't stop at Hayle."

"But if he got off here you must have seen him because it's the end the line. Unless of course the train was packed."

Anna sighed. "I know but sadly I didn't see him. There were a lot of people around though. You know, people meeting people as well as ones getting off the train, and he could have got off quicker than me especially if he wasn't burdened with luggage."

Poppy laughed. "I think it might be best if you forget all about him as the chance of ever seeing him again are extremely slim. A bit like looking for a needle in a haystack."

Anna sighed. "I know, and especially when I don't even know which haystack to look in. The thing is…that night I dreamt of him. I can't remember why or what part he played in my dream but that's why I've not been able to get his face out of my head. I see it all the time. You know, like when a tune gets stuck in your head."

Poppy picked up Anna's empty glass. "Poor you, I'll get you another glass of wine and then we'll talk about something else and see if we can put some different thoughts into your head."

"No, I'll get the drinks," said Anna, standing.

Poppy tutted. "Would that by any chance be so that you can take a peep round the corner while you're at the bar?"

Anna smiled sweetly. "In less than two days you've already learned to read me like a book, Poppy Templeton."

Chapter Four

When Anna went down for breakfast on Tuesday morning, the first person she saw was an unfamiliar man with a shock of thick blond hair which curled up on the collar of his black cotton shirt. His eyes were blue and he wore a pair of gold-rimmed spectacles perched on the end of his nose. Opposite him sat a woman with auburn hair piled up in an old-fashioned bun. Her back was towards the door and so Anna was unable to see her face in that instance. A smile lit up Anna's face as she crossed the room; they had to be Dominic the ghost hunter and his companion, Josephina.

Anna sat down at her usual table and subtly glanced over at the new arrivals who were deep in conversation, but she quickly averted her eyes when the female looked in her direction. Pretending to be lost in thought she fiddled with the paper napkin on her table until Michelle saved her embarrassment and arrived with her pot of tea.

As Anna poured her tea, fellow guest, Brenda caught her eye thus causing the pub landlady to rub her hands gleefully and nod in the direction of Dominic and Josephina. Anna giggled; Brenda was no doubt expecting to hear of great happenings once the ghost hunting began.

The vicar left the room and when Michelle began to clear his table, Anna asked her if Poppy was up.

"Just," said Michelle, placing dirty crockery onto a tray, "and at the moment she's out in the conservatory drinking coffee. You're very welcome to go and join her if you'd like to."

"Are you sure?" Anna asked, knowing that the conservatory was part of the family's private area.

"Of course," said Michelle. She pointed towards the door. "It's easy enough to find. From here go down the back corridor past the laundry room and past the old scullery. The conservatory door is half-glazed and you'll see it at the very end of the passage. You can't miss it."

Anna stood up. "Brilliant, I'll go there right away."

When Anna opened the conservatory door the bright sun shone straight into her eyes and dazzled her. With eyes squinted, she looked around for Poppy but was distracted by a large vine which stretched across the glass roof and dripped with ripening grapes.

As Anna rubbed her eyes in an attempt to acclimatise to the brightness, Poppy spoke.

"Morning Anna, have you seen the ghost hunters yet?"

Anna blinked as her vision cleared. "Yes, I saw them during breakfast and …."

Poppy leaned forward in her wicker chair. "What's the matter, Anna? You're gone as white as a sheet."

"Where…where, I don't understand…where's the vine gone?"

"Vine," said Poppy, with a laugh, "what vine?"

"In here, I just saw it. It was huge and dripping with purple grapes." Anna sat down before her legs gave way. "Am I going mad?"

As she spoke Michelle appeared with two slices of toast for Poppy. She immediately sensed something was amiss.

"What's the matter, girls?" she asked.

Poppy shook her head. "Anna appears to be hallucinating."

"I saw a grape vine," said Anna, on the verge of tears, "at least I thought I did. Admittedly my eyes were dazzled by the sun and so my sight was blurred, but it seemed real enough and was laden with grapes dangling from the roof in thick bunches."

Michelle handed the plate of toast to Poppy and then sat down. "Really? Now that is interesting. Weird too, I must admit. You see, there was an old grape vine in here when we first moved in. It was very old and woody, much of the main stem was dead and so it had very little life left in it. We took it out to do some repair work to the roof which leaked in several places. The back wall was in a bad way too."

Poppy's jaw dropped. "Is that right?"

Michelle nodded. "Yes, your dad and Alfie dug it out."

"Wow, that's creepy," said Poppy, taking a bite of toast. "Perhaps you have mystical powers, Anna. It might be worth telling Dominic when you get to know him and ask what he thinks."

Anna shuddered. "I'd rather not. From what I've seen I think he might give me the creeps. Anyway, I'm sure for some reason I must have imagined it. I mean, grapes often grow in conservatories, don't they? So maybe my subconscious expected me to see a huge vine and my imagination co-operated and went into overdrive. In fact, yes, of course, there's a grape vine in a huge conservatory on the back of the house next to the house in which we have our flat. We can see it clearly from our bedroom window, so that must be why my imagination got muddled."

"Hmm, I suppose that's as good a theory as any," said Poppy," clearly unconvinced.

Anna smiled. "Well, it's what I'm going to believe in order to keep my sanity. Although to be perfectly honest I've never encountered seeing things that aren't actually there before nor have I in the past had the ability to find my way around unfamiliar places. Not until I arrived in Cornwall, that is."

Poppy half-smiled. "Well, they do say that Cornwall is a mystical land of legends and myths, so perhaps for some reason you're susceptible to such things."

Michelle stood up. "Yes, who knows? That reminds me. Neither your dad nor I need the car today so if you want to go out somewhere sightseeing you're more than welcome to take it."

"Hmm, brilliant, yes," said Poppy, "we could go to Pentrillick. That's if you like, Anna. I've never been there before but Alfie's sister and her husband live in the village and his sister has a café there. It also has a really nice pub. We could have a wander round and then pop into the pub for lunch, coffee or whatever. What do you think?"

"Pentrillick, where's that?"

"It's not far away. I've seen it on a sign post between here and Helston. It's by the sea and Alfie raves about it. I'd like to go so I can tell him I've been because he's been saying for ages that I should."

Anna smiled. "I think that's a lovely idea. I was wondering what to do today and that would be perfect."

Poppy finished her toast and brushed crumbs from her lap. "Great, I just have a few jobs and then I'll be ready, so if you like I'll meet you in the guests' lounge at umm, say half eleven."

Anna nodded. "I'll be there."

"Brill," said Poppy, standing, "see you later."

"Yes, bye Poppy."

While Poppy was doing the rooms, Anna went outdoors to sit in the gardens. Alfie was trimming the tall privet hedge by the boundary wall at the foot of the lawn which ran alongside the road. He waved as she sat down beneath the apple tree to lap up the delights of another lovely day.

In the middle of the garden standing beside the pond, the vicar was speaking into his mobile phone. Poppy had told Anna that the vicar was down for an ecclesiastical meeting in Truro with which he was combining a short holiday. Anna watched as he finished his call and then headed back towards the house.

Pentrillick was only a few miles' drive from Penzance and like Penzance it lay on the south coast.

Poppy parked her parents' Audi in a small car park on the outskirts of the village and then they walked along the main street. After passing a school on their left they came across the pub, the Crown and Anchor which was situated on the opposite side to the school and so overlooked the sea. It was a large detached construction and built of granite. Hanging baskets and tubs of summer bedding brightened up the dark stone walls and a long wooden board bearing the pub's name ran above the door between the two rows of windows.

As they crossed the road to read the menu in a glass case beside the door, both girls agreed the pub no doubt looked much the same as it would have done when built in the early eighteen hundreds.

After reading the menu, they contemplated whether or not to go in for a coffee before they explored the village further, but decided instead to return to the pub for lunch and to have coffee in Alfie's sister's café instead, should they came across it.

They continued along the street and as they neared a church on the left hand side of the road, they saw the café, like the pub, on the same side as the sea."

"This must be it," said Poppy, glancing up at the board above the door saying Chloe's Café, "because Alfie's sister is called Chloe."

A middle-aged lady was clearing a table as they went in. "Good morning," she said with a welcoming smile.

"Hi, yes, good morning," said Poppy, "When you're ready may we have a couple of coffees, please?"

"Of course. Do take a seat wherever you like."

They sat down beside a window which looked out onto the street. Two other couples were already seated on opposite sides of the café. After loading up a tray with dirty crockery, the person clearing the table walked behind a counter and disappeared into a room beyond.

"Do you think she's Alfie's sister?" Anna whispered, nodding towards the back of the counter.

"I shouldn't think so," said Poppy, "I'm think she's too old. Alfie is thirty and I believe his sister is just a couple of years older than him, but I'll still ask."

As she spoke the woman in question returned with their coffees.

"Thank you," said Poppy, sweetly as the lady placed the cups with saucers on the table. "We were just wondering if you might be Alfie Trewin's sister."

The woman laughed. "I don't think Chloe would be very flattered if she heard you say that. She's a fair bit younger than me and a damn sight prettier too. I'm Louise and I work for Chloe. She's not here this morning though. She's gone to have her hair done."

"Oh, that's a shame," said Poppy, genuinely disappointed. "Alfie's been telling me for ages to come to Pentrillick and introduce myself."

"Are you a friend of his then?"

"Yes, he works for my mum and dad."

"Oh, so you live up at The Old Tile House, very nice too. Chloe has often said how good your folks are to her brother." She paused for a moment, clearly thinking, "You'll be the young lady that's at university then."

Poppy nodded. "Yes, that's me. Poppy by name and this is my friend, Anna."

"Poppy, that's a nice name. I'm very fond of poppies in fact I think they're probably my favourite flowers." She turned as two more people entered the café.

"Whoops, better go. Lovely to meet you both. I know Chloe will be sorry to have missed you when I tell her that you called."

Poppy frowned as Louise welcomed the newcomers. "I wish I didn't share my name with a flower," she grumbled, "it's so un-me."

"I think it's pretty," said Anna, "and so are all flower names."

"Humph, you would."

Noting that Poppy was serious, Anna tried not to laugh. "Don't you have a middle name that you could use instead?"

"I do but I don't like that either. It's Lee and I don't like it because there was a boy at junior school called Lee and he was a horrid little brat. Always teasing and boasting."

"Hmm, not very helpful then."

Poppy lifted up her cup of coffee and took a sip. "Do you have a middle name, Anna?"

Anna nodded. "Yes, it's Emily and I rather like it."

"Yes, that is nice. Annabelle Emily Greenwood. If it were possible I'd quite happily do a swap."

After leaving the café they continued to walk along the main street and out into the open countryside where they spotted a signpost pointing to the coastal path.

"Let's have a little wander," said Poppy, "We needn't go far, but just far enough to get the lay of the land."

After an hour of walking they both felt hungry and so decided to return to the Crown and Anchor for lunch.

"I feel all goosepimply," said Anna, as they entered the bar. "Like I did at St Michael's Mount. How weird."

Poppy took Anna by the arm. "Hopefully, that's because it feels chilly in here after being out in the sun and not because you're going all freaky on me again. Come on, let's get a drink and order some food and then we can go outside and gaze at the sea again."

As they walked through the French doors leading to the beer garden, Poppy saw a notice pinned on the wall. "Oh, now that's interesting," she said, pointing to the colourful sheet of laminated paper. "Pebbles and Sand are playing here on Saturday night, we really ought to come and see them."

"Pebbles and Sand," repeated Anna, "who or what might they be?"

"They're a covers band," said Poppy, "I've never actually seen them but I know Alfie has and he says they're fantastic. They're local too."

"Sounds good," said Anna, "and it would make a change to see a live band."

Poppy nodded. "I'll have a word with Alfie when we get back and if he's planning to see them then perhaps we can all come here together."

The beer garden terrace was raised up above sea level with a flight of ten steps leading down to the beach. Several round tables stood in the middle area and all around the edges beneath railings ran a wooden bench. Anna and Poppy sat at one of the tables where the sunshade was down so that they could feel the warmth of the sun.

There was no-one in the sea and just a lone walker strolling across the sand with a dog. Further along, where the beach ended with cliffs jutting out to sea, two men sat on rocks beneath the cliff face with fishing rods cast into the calm water.

Anna rested her elbows on the table and leaned her face into her cupped hands. "I love the sound of the sea, it's so soothing. Were I to live somewhere like this I don't think I'd ever tire of hearing it, or seeing it either for that matter."

Poppy cast her eyes towards the shore. "Yes, I agree and I love it when it's rough too. When I came home last Christmas there were a couple of storms and so I went with Alfie down town to watch the sea. It was crazy and at high water it was crashing up over the promenade. It was really exciting; breathtaking too."

"Hard to imagine it being rough on a day like this," said Anna, dreamily. "You're so lucky, Poppy having somewhere like Cornwall to call home."

"Yes, I suppose I am. And at the moment I have the best of both worlds. A hectic social life in a city while at uni and the peace of Cornwall when I come home."

Before they prepared to leave, Poppy stood up. "I must pop to the loo, I wonder where it is?"

"It's at the far end of the bar opposite the door leading into the dining room," said Anna. "There's a brass plaque saying: *Yer Tiz, Ladies,* on the door, you can't miss it."

Poppy frowned. "How do you know that?"

"What? ...Oh, I...I really don't know. Perhaps I'm wrong." Anna shuddered, "Oh dear God, please may I be wrong."

Poppy wandered to the end of the bar and followed Anna's directions. When she returned she looked concerned. "You were spot on, Anna. Are you sure you haven't been here before. With your mother perhaps. Maybe you mixed up Devon and Cornwall when you were a child. It's easy for memories to get muddled."

Anna shook her head. "No, Mum and I definitely never came to Cornwall. It was a sort of joke we shared and I never went on holiday with anyone else. Besides, having no family apart from Mum there was no-one else to go with."

In the evening, Anna went into the guests' lounge where she and Poppy were to meet prior to going out for a drink and meeting up with Alfie and some of his friends. To her delight, the ghost hunter and his girlfriend were in there talking with Brian and Brenda.

"Ah, Anna," said Brian, as she closed the door, "Have you met the new guests?"

"No, no I haven't, but I did see them at breakfast." She nodded politely to the new-comers.

"Then come over here, dear," said Brenda, standing and beckoning her to step forwards, "and we'll introduce you."

Anna did as she was asked.

"Right, now Dominic, Jo," said Brian, to the couple who were seated on the small settee, "this lovely young lady is Anna Greenwood. And Anna, these charming and incredibly interesting people are Dominic and Jo."

"Pleased to meet you," said Anna, smiling at each new guest in turn.

"The pleasure is all mine," said Dominic, standing and taking a bow before he kissed her hand which he held tightly between his long fingers.

"And I'm pleased to meet you too," said Josephina, with considerably less show as she remained seated.

"Dominic is a ghost hunter," said Brenda, in awe, "and he's going ghost hunting on Friday night in a spooky old castle. Isn't that exciting?"

Anna smiled and frowned at the same time. "Yes, so I've heard but I'm not really sure whether I think it's exciting or not. I mean, it's certainly different but I don't think it would suit me as I'm inclined to jump out of my skin at any sudden noise."

"Oh, it's fun," said Josephina, with a childlike giggle. "Dom sees all sorts of things that I don't but then that's because he's super intelligent and sensitive to such things." She gazed at him adoringly.

"Come, come now, Josephina, let us not exaggerate. Certainly my gifts are extraordinary but that cannot be attributed to intelligence alone but more to being in tune with one's inner self and the spiritual world that surrounds one."

As Dominic was speaking, Anna found herself mesmerised by his slightly unusual appearance. For apart from a colourful brocade waistcoat, he was dressed from head to toe in black which made his pale skin seem almost white. The spectacles he had worn during breakfast were now dangling from a gold chain around his neck, and his piercing, blue eyes seemed to search her soul. She shuddered and felt in desperate need of making her exit. To her relief the door opened and Poppy peeped into the room.

Anna looked pleadingly at her friend. "Poppy you must come in and meet your new guests."

"We've already met," said Dominic, stepping forward to kiss Poppy's hand. "We were introduced by this young lady's lovely mother a short while ago."

"Yep, that's right," said Poppy, in a polite yet very down-to-earth manner.

Anna picked up her handbag from the arm of the settee where she had dropped it.

Poppy backed towards the door. "Are you ready then, Anna? I feel in need of a nice cold pint of Stella."

"Yes, yes, I'm ready." She turned to Dominic and Josephina. "Lovely to have met you and I don't doubt that I'll see you both tomorrow at breakfast." She smiled at Brenda and Brian. "And you too of course."

"Well, what do you think of them?" Poppy asked as they left the house and walked down the winding driveway.

"Bizarre, both of them," said Anna, glad to be outside. "They make a very odd couple and I thought he was rather creepy."

"Hmm, yes, I agree, and I don't buy that ghost nonsense. I think he's just a born showoff and she's smitten by his crazy antics."

"His behaviour is rather over the top, I must admit. Do you think he's really like that or is it all an act?"

"An act no doubt but I can't see why he bothers. I hardly think anyone will be impressed down here."

Anna agreed. "Hmm, I found him quite formidable. On the other hand perhaps he's really shy or something like that and puts on an act because he doesn't like being himself."

Poppy frowned. "He's more likely to be a serial killer who behaves as he does so that he is completely the opposite of any descriptions put out about him."

Anna laughed. "I think perhaps you might watch too much television, Poppy."

"Actually, my thoughts are inspired by the book I'm currently reading. It's a very dark, murder mystery and Dominic reminds me of the bad guy in it."

Chapter Five

Anna woke up on Wednesday morning with a throbbing headache and groaned when she remembered that she was supposed to be going surfing. Feeling too fragile to shower, she dressed slowly and then went down for breakfast hoping a cup of tea might help clear her head.

Inside the morning room, only the vicar was seated. Poppy, up bright and early because of the day out, was waiting at the tables. She stopped dead in her tracks when she saw Anna's pale face.

"Oh, my goodness, are you alright, Anna? You look awful."

Anna half smiled. "I feel awful." She sat down. "Regrettably I have a rotten headache."

Poppy sat down on the chair opposite Anna. "Would you like me to get you something for it?"

Anna nodded. "Yes, no, I mean yes. Oh dear." She sighed feebly, "I'm sorry for sounding such an idiot, the thing is I can't swallow tablets whole and so only ever take dispersible aspirin when at home. You probably think me a bit odd but I have a fear of choking, you see."

Poppy smiled. "Don't worry, you're not alone. Mum is exactly the same and so we have medicines here to cure all ills."

Anna looked relieved. "In that case, yes please. I really would appreciate something."

While Poppy was in the kitchen rummaging through the medicine cabinet, Dominic and Josephina entered the morning room. Dominic bowed to Anna as he greeted her. Josephina smiled. The vicar looked over the rim of his coffee mug and scowled at everyone.

Poppy looked a little downcast as she handed Anna a glass of water fizzing with two effervescent aspirin. "Will you still be able to come surfing?"

Anna shook her head. "I really don't think it would be a very good idea as I'm feeling a little nauseous too. I imagine surfing is pretty strenuous and never having been before I think it might be pushing myself a bit too far. I'm sorry, but I think it would be best if you went without me, although I hate to be such a wet blanket."

"That's such a shame, but..."

"No buts," said Anna, "please go. It's only fair to Alfie and it is his day off."

"Are you sure?"

"Of course," said Anna, "I shall have a lazy day and if I feel a bit better later I might take a walk down to the beach."

Poppy picked up the empty medicine glass. "Okay and I really do hope you're feeling better soon."

Anna smiled. "Thank you," she said, but then frowned, "I hope you don't think I'm making the headache up as an excuse not to go to Newquay."

Poppy shook her head. "No, I don't. That is unless you have a talent for doing theatrical make-up which can make a usually healthy face look as sick as a parrot."

Anna attempted to laugh which made her headache feel worse. "Ouch, I shall miss you and your sense of humour today."

"And I shall miss you appreciating it."

After breakfast, Anna, having asked Poppy not to bother doing her room when she did the others, slept for an hour. When she awoke her head ached a little less and so she took a shower and then made her bed.

Poppy and Alfie had already left for Newquay when she went downstairs and so she did as planned and walked down to the beach hoping the fresh air might help to clear her head completely. Rafe, always glad of a walk, accompanied her after she had first asked Michelle for permission to take him out.

The beach lay calm and would have been desolate were it not for a few late season holiday makers flying two kites in the distance towards Marazion. Anna, with Rafe by her side, slowly walked along the compressed wet sand towards the kite flyers, eagerly searching for somewhere to sit. The tide was almost at its lowest ebb and near to the coastline a flock of gulls swarmed and squawked above a small inshore fishing boat.

Between the sea and the coastal path, piles of large boulders deposited as a defence against the sea during storms, edged the top of the beach. When she felt they had walked far enough, Anna stopped and selected the flattest, smoothest one she could find and then sat down delighted to feel the warmth from the boulder through her jeans, no doubt radiated by the sun.

As she opened up her Kindle, a train tooted on its approach to the level crossing beside the car park at Long Rock. Anna turned her head but was too low down to catch even a glimpse of the train.

Meanwhile Rafe, after sniffing around, settled down by her feet where he eyed a piece of dry seaweed caught on a lump of rotting driftwood as it fluttered in the breeze. After a while he lost interest in the seaweed and with his eyes closed appeared to be sleeping.

An hour peacefully passed by and then for no apparent reason, Anna suddenly felt cold. She shivered, puzzled by the sudden chill which seemed peculiar as the sun was still shining brightly. She stood up, rubbed her arms to dispel the goose pimples and then glanced down at Rafe who was growling softly by her feet.

"What's the matter, Rafe?" she asked, gently stroking his warm head.

Rafe continued to growl and then suddenly he jumped up and barked.

Anna panicked. "What's wrong? You're frightening me. Stop it. There's no-one here, Rafe. It's just you and me."

Rafe's barking stopped as abruptly as it began and to Anna's relief he sat back down beside their footprints in the sand. Still feeling shaken, Anna resumed her position on the rock, but as she lifted up her Kindle, she noticed that their two sets of footprints were not alone. Another set of prints had emerged - prints larger than those made by Anna and Rafe. Yet they all stopped close together, at the same spot, next to the rocks where they sat.

Anna closed her Kindle and dropped it onto the rocks, she then knelt down beside Rafe. Confused by the footprints, she cast her eyes along the beach. No-one else was visible other than the holiday makers in the distance with the kites.

As she reached out to touch the mysterious set of prints, the sudden roar of a motorbike engine shattered the peace. Anna, alarmed, jumped and turned towards the small car park which lay behind the beach. To her annoyance, a scruffy looking man sat astride a mud-splattered bike drinking water from a plastic bottle.

He nodded. "Nice day."

Anna frowned. "Yes," she replied, aware of the cold anger in her voice.

With his eyes firmly fixed on her face, he ran his fingers through his untidy blond hair and then tucked the bottle inside the pocket his shabby, leather jacket. "Better be off or I'll have the boss after me," he said, and with a nod of his head, he roared back through the car park towards the level-crossing and the road.

Listlessly, Anna sat down on the sand and clumsily stroked Rafe who laid his head on her lap. She had never liked motor bikes: nasty, noisy things. Her head began to ache again and she felt a strong desire to cry.

Anna was in the guests' lounge, playing cards and drinking wine again with Brian and Brenda when Poppy and Alfie returned from Newquay.

"How are you feeling, Anna?" Poppy asked, after opening the lounge door and peeping into the room.

"Fine, thanks. The headache went off several hours ago. Have you had a good day?"

"Brilliant. I'm just popping upstairs for a shower then I'll see you later."

"Will you join us for a game or two?" Brian eagerly asked.

Poppy paused in the doorway. "Yes, yes, I think I will. It'll be nice to sit down for a while. I must admit my legs are aching."

"And you must have a glass or two of wine as well," said Brenda, nodding towards the bottles on the sideboard.

"Hmm, lovely that would slip down nicely." She looked further into the room and whispered, "Are the ghost hunters not in here?"

Brenda shook her head. "No, I was talking to Jo earlier and she said they were going out for a meal tonight. Which is a shame as I was hoping to get Dominic drinking wine so it'd loosen his tongue and then I could badger him into telling of some ghostly experiences."

Poppy giggled. "Oh, dear. Poor you. So what do you make of them?"

"Jo is very nice. Intelligent and chatty," said Brenda. "But as I indicated just now, Dominic doesn't say much and seems to be more of an observer. I think he seems a bit creepy too." She gasped unexpectedly. "Oh dear, I do hope he's not a mind-reader."

Poppy smiled. "Yeah, I've noticed he's quiet. Anyway, must go, be back in a jiffy."

"Do you really think Dominic is quiet?" Anna asked as Poppy left the room and closed the door behind her. "I thought he seemed to have plenty to say."

"Certainly he did yesterday," said Brenda, "but he seems to have gone a lot quieter today. You know, more thoughtful like."

"A bit like the vicar," said Brian, with a chuckle, "I can't seem to get a word out of him."

"Does he ever come in here?" asked Anna, "The vicar, I mean."

"We've seen him once or twice but he always leaves when we get the cards and wine out so he probably disapproves," said Brenda. "Not that we ever gamble. Not on cards anyway. In fact, our gambling habits go no further than raffle tickets and the National Lottery."

"And we never seem to win anything on them," Brian gruffly added.

Brenda nodded. "No, but then it's nice to know we're helping the many good causes."

After her shower, Poppy when invited to do so, poured herself a glass of wine and then took a seat at the table opposite Anna. "Right, what are we playing?" she asked, flicking a strand of damp hair from her eyes.

"We were playing rummy," said Brenda, "but we can play something else if you prefer."

Poppy bit her bottom lip. "To be honest I don't really know any card games other than snap. Can you teach me?"

"Of course," said Brian, "we'd be delighted."

As he started to explain the game, Anna rose from her chair. "While you're doing this, I'll just pop up to the loo. Won't be a minute."

Poppy was quick to comprehend the simple rules of rummy and so while waiting for Anna to return, asked the Cookes how they were enjoying their break.

"Very much," said Brenda, with enthusiasm, "but I'm a little worried about your new friend, Anna."

"Anna," said Poppy, "why?"

"Well, just before you got back she was telling us about her visit to the beach today. Apparently while she was sitting on some rocks, Rafe started barking and then she noticed there was another set of footprints alongside those of herself and the dog. I don't think she would have mentioned it had she not had a couple of glasses of wine but she seemed quite put out by it, didn't she, Brian?"

"Yes, she did," Brian agreed.

Poppy frowned. "But surely the footprints might already have been there and she just hadn't seen them."

Brian drained his glass and then nodded. "I agree and I said as much to the lass." He stood up and walked over to the sideboard. "But I don't think she was very convinced."

"And that's not all," said Brenda, "She said she keeps getting feelings of déjà vu even though she's never been to Cornwall before. So what do you think might be the cause of that?"

Poppy frowned. "Yes, I know because I've been with her when she's had these weird feelings. In fact only yesterday we went to Pentrillick. I don't know whether you know it but it's a village just along the coast from here. It's very picturesque and Alfie's sister has a café there."

Brenda and Brian both nodded. "We went out there a couple of days ago," said Brenda, "and very nice it is too. We didn't know that young Alfie's sister had a café there though."

"But then that's because we didn't even know that Alfie had a sister," added Brian.

Poppy smiled, amused by the scornful look on Brian's face. "Yes, she does and it's called Chloe's Café. Anyway, we went in the pub there for lunch and before we left I said I must go to the loo. Anna told me where it was even though she says she's never been there before in her life. She even knew there was a brass plaque on the door saying *Yer Tiz, Ladies*."

Brenda opened her mouth to answer but quickly closed it when she heard Anna walking down the stairs.

That night when Anna went to her room she attempted to push all of the day's unsavoury thoughts from her mind and focus instead on the fun she'd had playing cards. After all, the young man on the motor bike must surely have meant her no harm and nothing was to be gained from dwelling on an over active imagination. And as for the footprints, perhaps Brian was right and they had been there all along. Yet sleep did not come easily as she snuggled down beneath the white duvet, and when finally she did succumb, it brought no respite. In her dreams she was frantically running across a beach littered with gigantic footprints and behind her was an enormous motor bike trying to run her down driven by Andy, her teddy bear.

Chapter Six

Anna laughed out loud on Thursday morning when she awoke and saw Andy sitting on her pillow for he reminded her of the dream. After reprimanding him for riding a dangerous motor bike, she stepped from her bed determined to approach the day with a positive attitude.

Before going down for breakfast she took a shower and as she dried herself she noticed that her nail varnish was badly chipped on two of her fingers. Thinking it unsightly, she resolved to remove it and apply a fresh coat. However, when she looked through her cosmetic bag for her nail polish remover she remembered it was still on top of the bedside table in the flat she shared with her work colleagues. Tutting, she decided that she must walk into town straight after breakfast and buy a new bottle.

As the guests sat in the morning room during breakfast, James popped his head around the doorframe. "Ah, you are here," he said looking at Brian and Brenda. "Just wondered if you fancy a game or two of tennis this morning, Brian. The bloke I normally play with has broken his thumb and so can't play. But the court is booked and it seems a shame to waste it."

"Dear oh dear," said Brian, "poor chap. Yes, I'd love a game. Make a nice change, but I don't have any racquets with me."

"No need to worry about that, I've a shelf full of them upstairs so you can take your pick."

"Ideal, so what time are you thinking of going?"

"About eleven if that's alright with you."

"That's fine, and Brenda can come along as well and be our ball girl."

Brenda groaned. "I'd rather be the umpire."

Anna enjoyed browsing through the shops in Penzance and as well as buying nail polish remover she also bought a new dress and nail varnish to match the diagonal stripes on her new garment.

Further along the street, in the window of a charity shop, she saw a Toby jug and so went inside to take a closer look. Amused by the expression on the face of the jug's character, she bought it for Michelle, reasoning that if Michelle already had one like it then she would keep it for herself.

After leaving the shopping area she walked down towards the coast and then strolled along the promenade towards Wherrytown.

Warmed by her walk, she paused to unbutton her jacket and take a rest on a bench which faced out to sea, but as she sat she felt that she was being watched. Slowly she turned her head, but no-one was close by or even looking in her direction. Turning back towards the sea she acknowledged that she must have been mistaken. But then the feeling returned: the feeling of eyes piercing the back of her neck. Quickly she turned her head hoping to catch out whoever was watching her, but again there was no-one there. She rose steadily from the bench and looked back and forth along the promenade and then over the road to the buildings on the other side. There were a few people about but no-one was looking her way.

Feeling silly Anna decided to return to The Old Tile House where she hoped Poppy would be out and about, for she knew her friend's down-to-earth manner would soon quash any notions she had of someone watching her.

On her way back to the guest house, Anna bought two bottles of merlot, as she wanted to make a contribution to the sideboard in the guests' lounge. She also bought some peanuts and a multipack bag of crisps.

Poppy was in the garden idly watching Alfie digging up wallflower plants from the nursery bed ready to transfer to the spring flower border, when Anna arrived back at The Old Tile House. Hoping to get Poppy and Alfie's approval, Anna showed them both her new dress and then took it indoors and hung it in the wardrobe. While in her room, she decided quickly to remove her chipped nail varnish, but did not apply a new coat as she was keen to get back outside.

The smell of fish and chips tantalised her sense of smell as she descended the stairs. At the bottom she met Roger the vicar with sunglasses perched on top of his thick head of hair. He had a polystyrene tray clutched in one hand and a few chips gripped in the other. Anna smiled sweetly and he nodded in response, she then went outside to where Poppy was telling Alfie that later in the day two more guests were due to arrive and they were magicians.

"Magicians," laughed Alfie, putting the last of the wallflowers into a trug, "good heavens, what a strange collection of guests you currently have. Ghost hunters, magicians and a dodgy vicar."

"Dodgy vicar," repeated Anna, on hearing the conversation. "What's dodgy about him?"

Alfie laughed. "Well, on Sunday morning he went off down the drive on foot. I said 'off to church, Vicar,' and he said 'yes, my son,' which I thought was a hoot, him being a similar age to me."

Poppy frowned. "But that doesn't make him dodgy."

Alfie shook his finger. "Ah, but there's more. In the evening I went out to the pub with my mates and while we were in the games room playing pool I saw him sitting in the bar chatting up some female. And, this is the main thing, he wore a lightweight scarf round his neck which covered up his dog collar, so I reckon he didn't want her to know that he was a man of the cloth."

Poppy laughed. "Perhaps he is an interesting vicar after all. What was he drinking? Don't tell me it was Jagerbombs."

Alfie laughed. "No, definitely not. It looked like he was on the real ale."

"Hmm, does sound a little odd," Anna agreed, "Covering his collar, I mean, not the beer drinking."

"Anyway, that's enough about the vicar," said Alfie, "I'm more interested in the magicians. So what can you tell us about them, Poppy?"

Poppy shrugged her shoulders. "Very little really, other than that there are two of them, a bloke and a woman. I believe he's the magician and she is his assistant. Something like that."

"And are they famous?" Anna asked, hopefully.

"No idea," said Poppy, "I don't even know what they're called but we'll no doubt find out later."

"Hmm, food for thought," said Alfie, picking up the trug, "perhaps we can get him to magic the apples off the tree to save James and me having to get the cumbersome ladder out."

"You don't need magic for that," said Poppy, "or a ladder, a good old gusty wind will save you the bother."

Alfie looked heavenwards. "Trust you to opt for the easy way out, Poppy. No consideration at all for the fact the poor apples will get bruised that way."

Poppy tutted. "Well, I don't suppose they'll care about that since they're going to be eaten and will end up at the sewage treatment plant anyway."

"Yuck, that's gross," said Anna, shaking her head.

After a three set tennis match which Brian won with ease, James, Brian and Brenda went into the club's café for a drink.

"Well, I must admit you're marvellous for your age, Brian," said James, as he placed drinks on the table, "I never dreamed you'd beat me, especially that easily."

"He plays a lot at home," said Brenda, taking a sip of her gin and tonic, "and has done so since before we met and that's over forty two years ago now."

James shook his head. "Practise certainly makes perfect then. You must be a good twenty years my senior."

"I'll be sixty nine in December," said Brian.

"And I turned sixty five last month," added Brenda, "not that that has any relevance to Brian's ability to play tennis."

James tutted. "Oh dear, more than a twenty year age gap then as I'm just a boy at forty five."

"Oh, to be forty five again," groaned Brian.

"Does Michelle play tennis at all?" Brenda asked.

James shook his head. "No, she's into Pilates and stuff like that."

"Very wise. We go ballroom dancing as often as we can. Brian won't tell you so himself, but he's very good at dancing."

Brian patted his flat stomach. "Yes, that and the tennis helps keep me fit."

"And I should imagine having a pub keeps you on your toes too. I know running a guest house does."

"Absolutely," said Brian, "we don't have any letting rooms at our current pub but we have had in the past so know of the work involved."

"Have you and Michelle lived at The Old Tile House long?" Brenda asked.

"No, in fact little more than a year. We used to live in Wiltshire and ran a guest house there. We came down here simply because we fancied a change of scenery and when we saw The Old Tile House we knew we'd done the right thing. I love the place and so does Michelle."

"It certainly has heaps of character," said Brenda. "How many actual letting rooms do you have?"

"Six," said Brian, "one single, one twin, three double and a family room which sleeps four."

"So you're nearly full," said Brenda, doing a quick tot up on her fingers.

"Yes, we've a new couple arriving this afternoon and then only the family room will be free."

"How exciting," said Brenda, "I love it when new guests arrive, especially if they're a bit different like Dominic."

James laughed. "Yes, Dominic certainly is a character. I get the feeling he thinks the house is haunted though judging by the amount of times I see him deep in concentration with his eyes closed."

"Is there any reason for the house to have a ghost?" Brenda asked. "I mean, has anyone tragically died there or anything like that?"

James shrugged his shoulders. "Not to my knowledge and the people we bought the house from never mentioned a ghost and they'd been there a fair number of years. Getting on for twenty in fact."

"I think it's all poppycock," said Brian, "and I think Dominic and Jo are barmy opting to spend a night in a draughty old castle when they could be nicely tucked up in a comfortable warm bed."

James nodded. "I'm inclined to agree with you there."

Brenda frowned. "What a couple of killjoys you are."

In the very early hours of Friday morning, Anna awoke for no apparent reason. As she blinked to adjust her eyes to the darkness, she sensed movement and heard a strange noise. Quickly she sat up and switched on the bedside lamp but there was no-one in the room and nothing to indicate what the noise might have been. Feeling anything but brave she slipped out of bed and looked into the bathroom thinking something might have fallen down. But again there was nothing out of place. Feeling chilled as well nervous she climbed back into bed and looked at the clock on the bedside table; it was half past two. For five minutes she sat and listened for any further sounds with Andy clutched on her arms, but all was quiet. Thinking she must have imagined the noise or have been dreaming, she switched off the lamp and snuggled back beneath the bedclothes.

Chapter Seven

On Friday morning Anna woke up and instantly remembered the strange noise she'd heard in the early hours and the movement she had sensed. But she quickly pushed that feeling of unease to one side when she recalled having just dreamt of the man on the train again.

She sighed deeply and tried hard to relive her dream during which the man from the train had been seated on a green, iron bench. Her mouth turned upside-down as she recalled that he was crying and wiping tears from his eyes with a large white handkerchief. Puzzled, Anna paused momentarily, she then slipped out of bed and went over to the window to see what the morning held from a meteorological point of view. To her dismay it was raining.

Once she was dressed and ready for breakfast, she picked up the key of her room from the bedside cabinet and dropped it into the pocket of her jeans, but as she walked towards the door and reached out for the handle she saw something shining on the floor. She bent forward and picked the object up. It was a small red shank button with a diamanté centre. Clutching it in her hand, she opened up her wardrobe door and looked through her garments hanging from the rail even though she already knew that none of her clothes had buttons as elaborate as the one she had found.

Feeling a little anxious she closed the wardrobe doors and sat down on the bed. Where had the button come from? She was convinced it had not been there the day before as she would have noticed it when she had entered or left the room. She shuddered. Perhaps after all there had been someone in her room during the night. But how could anyone have got in when the door was locked? It was obvious all of the rooms had spare keys for Poppy would need them to clean the rooms, but surely no-one else would have access to them. Anna stood up; she must keep alert. Meanwhile she would look for someone wearing a garment with a button missing.

When Anna entered the morning room for breakfast, she saw there were two unfamiliar faces sitting at the table nearest the door. Brenda nodded towards them with her eyebrows raised when she caught Anna's eye. Both then smiled. Clearly they were the magician and his assistant, for he wore a red jacket covered in large gold stars and she wore skimpy shorts and a bat-winged top smothered in sequins.

"They're called Meldrick and Maci," said Poppy, when she met Anna at the foot of the stairs later in the morning, "but Mum said Meldrick must be his stage name because the room was booked in the name of Colin Davenport. I don't know if Maci is her real name."

"So what do they want to be known as?" Anna asked.

"Meldrick and Maci, I assume. That's what they introduced themselves as to Mum and Dad anyway."

"Any idea why they're here? I mean, are they performing somewhere in the area or what?"

"No, they're just taking a break. Apparently they've been on tour for much of the summer and finished the season in Plymouth last weekend. They stayed in Newquay for a couple of nights after leaving Plymouth and now they've come down here because they think it might be nice and peaceful."

"Hmm, yes it is, but also this morning it's wet. What do people do in Penzance when it's raining?"

Poppy shrugged her shoulders. "Much the same as anywhere else I suppose. What do you normally do on wet days?"

Anna sighed. "Well, were I home the chances are I'd be working, but if not I could explore museums or galleries, go shopping or visit one of the numerous tourist attractions, go and see an exhibition, there's always one on somewhere and then of course I could go and see a show. There are several I've not seen yet."

"Oh," said Poppy lost for words, "um, well there must be something we can do here."

"You can tidy the office if you like," said Michelle, appearing in the hallway, "it's in a shocking state. Your dad keeps saying he'll do it but he never seems to find the time. You were always very good at tidying up when you were younger because you hated things out of order. What was it you used to say?"

"A place for everything and everything in its place," said Poppy, with a scowl, "it was what Granny instilled into me when she came to stay once upon a time. She helped me tidy my bedroom and showed me the importance of being methodical. I've never forgotten it."

"Exactly," said Michelle, "but for some reason she never got that message over to her son."

Poppy smiled. "Yes, I agree, Dad's not very tidy. So what's he doing today?"

"He's gone with Alfie to look at floor tiles because the ones in the old scullery are badly cracked in places."

"Oh." Poppy turned to Anna. "Do you fancy helping me tidy the office? It shouldn't take too long."

"Yes, why not. It'll make a change but you'll have to tell me what to do."

"No need to be too thorough," said Michelle, leading the girls down the hallway towards the office where she opened the door, "it'd just be nice to have it tidy especially the desk, so that I can find things."

"Leave it to us," said Poppy, entering the room and eying the mess, "we'll have it done it a jiffy."

"Thank you, I really do appreciate it," said Michelle. With a thumbs up sign, she left the room and closed the door.

While Poppy tidied up books, files and papers on shelves, Anna tackled the mess on the window seat which was completely hidden beneath a mass of newspapers, plastic folders, computer printouts and old photographs. After separating things she bundled them together with similar items and stacked them neatly. She took very little notice of the photographs until she came across one of The Old Tile House. She held it up for Poppy to see. "Any idea when was this taken?" Anna asked.

Poppy took the picture from Anna. "Must be just after we first moved here because the gardens are badly overgrown. Look, there's Dad with his arms folded over by the weeping willow so I daresay the photo was taken by Mum." She turned the picture over and looked at the back. "October 2012. So yes, it was taken just after Mum and Dad moved in."

Anna looked over Poppy's shoulder. "I'm beginning to get my bearings now. So if that's the weeping willow which is by the pond, where is the pond or did your dad and Alfie make it?"

"No, it was definitely already here because Alfie told me they had to clear it out because it was completely hidden, so it must be beneath this mess," she said pointing to a mass of weeds and brambles. "I know Alfie said it was more like a bog than a pond and needless to say there were no fish."

"Hmm, yes, that looks about the right place," Anna agreed, "but where's the summerhouse?"

"This would have been taken before the summer house was built because I remember Dad and Alfie doing that during the Christmas holiday last year when I was home from uni."

Poppy handed the picture back to Anna who studied it further. "What a transformation," she said, "Were it not for the house and its chimneys I don't think I would even have recognised it."

Anna was about to add the photograph to the rest of the pile when she became aware of a person she'd not noticed before. "Ah, who is this?" she asked Poppy, pointing to a face of a young woman amongst the shrubs.

Poppy shook her head. "Really, I've no idea. Whoever it is appears to be on the driveway so it's probably some girl delivering leaflets or something like that and she just happened to look through the shrubs as the picture was taken. It's certainly no-one I know anyway."

"Hmm, sounds feasible, I suppose." Anna placed the picture on top of the photograph pile.

"On the other hand," said Poppy, with a giggle, "perhaps it's the ghost of someone who once lived here and she had dropped by to see if the new residents met with her approval."

"Better not show it to Dominic then," said Anna, with a laugh, as she picked up the pile of photographs and placed them into a clear plastic wallet.

Inside the guests' lounge, Michelle, who was delighted with the Toby jug that Anna had found in the charity shop, decided that before she added it to her collection she must remove all the jugs from the shelves and give them a thorough dusting. When the job was done, she fetched the vacuum cleaner from the cupboard beneath the stairs and vacuumed the floor. And because she had plenty of time and knew all the guests were out, except Anna who was tidying the office with Poppy, she also removed the scatter cushions from the settees and armchairs and vacuumed down the back of the seating.

Suddenly the cleaner stopped sucking and made a horrible screeching noise. Michelle switched the machine off and pushed her hand down the back of the settee. To her surprise she found a credit card bearing the name Shane Scully. Michelle sat down and tried to recall any recent guests of that name and because no-one sprang to mind she assumed it must have been someone whose stay was brief and his name therefore had not imprinted itself on her brain. Tucking the card inside her pocket she continued with the cleaning.

Because they ran a pub, Brian and Brenda Cooke were used to eating meals at irregular times and as old habits die hard they chose to continue with the irregularity during their holiday in Cornwall. When they were at home they would have been working through lunchtime, so each day they left The Old Tile House for a walk around Penzance, where they looked at the shops, visited galleries, strolled around gardens or sauntered along the promenade. Then after their bouts of exercise they would go to the first pub or licensed restaurant they came across for a very late lunch.

On Friday they decided to do something a little different and so despite the rain they left earlier than usual and caught the branch line train to St. Ives where they viewed the galleries and shops. Had the weather been good they would have walked along the extensive beach, but, as it was, the beach was deserted except for the occasional gull and a lone walker dressed in Wellington boots and raincoat.

When they were hungry they went into a pub for lunch. It was packed with people glad to get out of the rain. They ordered fish and chips because that's what the people on the next table were eating and the smell was tantalising.

After leaving the pub they walked beneath their umbrellas down a narrow alleyway and as they passed the back of a commercial building Brian saw Roger the vicar from The Old Tile House huddled in a doorway with another man and both were smoking cigarettes. To Brian's surprise, when the vicar spotted Brenda and himself, he quickly snatched the cigarette from the mouth from the other man and dropped it along with his own beneath the soles of his boots. He then nodded politely to Brian and Brenda as they passed by.

"Did you see that?" Brian said when they were out of earshot.

"See what?" Brenda asked, her attention taken by a colourful display of hanging baskets.

"The vicar and the bloke with him, they were both smoking fags but when Roger saw us he chucked both fags on the ground and stamped on them."

"Probably didn't want us to see that he smoked," said Brenda, stepping aside to avoid water gushing from a piece of broken guttering, "he might think it ungodly or something like that."

"No, there's nothing wrong with a vicar having a fag. If you remember our one back home was a regular smoker until he gave up last year."

"So what are you implying?"

"Whacky baccy," said Brian, "that's what."

Early on Friday evening, Anna and Poppy sat in the guests' lounge chatting to Brenda and Brian who were glad to be back in the warm after a day in the rain. Also in the lounge were the latest arrivals, Meldrick and Maci, who to the delight of their fellow guests performed card tricks and entertained with amusing repartee. Meanwhile, Dominic and Josephina prepared to leave The Old Tile House to spend the night ghost hunting at Pengersick Castle. Before they left they popped into the lounge to say goodbye to their fellow guests.

"I do hope it's stopped raining," said Brenda, "otherwise you might get very cold and damp."

Brian tutted. "I'm pretty sure the castle will have a roof, Brenda, so no need to fret."

"Well, of course I know it'll have a roof but I was meaning…oh, never mind."

Anna caught a glimpse of equipment stacked in the hallway. "Whatever is all that stuff for?"

"Oh, all sorts of things," said Josephina, clearly excited. "There's an electronic thermometer to register when the temperature drops, a night vision camera to take pictures in the dark, and an audio recorder for obvious reasons: plus a few other gadgets that I'm not really sure what they do."

Dominic tutted. "Women."

Brenda felt her heart quicken. "I do hope you'll be alright. Half of me envies you both but the other half feels quite anxious. Do take care, won't you?"

Josephina smiled. "We'll be okay. There will be quite a few of us and ghosts are seldom aggressive anyway."

"Yes, I'm sure you're right, but you might encounter a poltergeist," said Brenda, "and I believe they can be quite bad tempered."

"Certainly such phenomena can be a little mischievous, noisy too," said Dominic, "but I think it highly unlikely we'll be bothered by any tonight."

Josephina giggled. "Shame really, because there's no mistaking them when they get up to their tricks."

Dominic shook his head and tutted. "Come along, Josephina or we shall be late. Goodbye everyone."

The remaining guests waved and then watched as the two ghost hunters picked up their equipment and left by the front door. Josephina, fearing it might be cold in the dead of night, was wearing a thick coat, gloves and a woolly hat. Dominic, on the other hand was dressed for show and wore a black, knee length cape and a deer stalker hat.

"Sherlock Holmes didn't go ghost hunting, did he?" Maci asked, as they heard Dominic's car engine start.

Poppy laughed. "Not to my knowledge. I think Dominic just likes to be different."

Brenda poured herself a glass of wine and then sat down on the small settee. "Hmm, he certainly is a bit of a showoff, but I can't help but like him."

"Anyway, he's gone now," said Brian, sitting down beside his wife, "so how about a few more card tricks, Meldrick?"

"My pleasure," said the magician, picking up the pack of cards and skilfully shuffling them.

Anna and Poppy had planned to go out later in the evening but after meeting Meldrick and Maci they had decided to stay as they enjoyed their company and that of Brian and Brenda too. Meldrick entertained them with numerous card tricks which left them speechless. None of the spectators had the slightest idea of how the tricks were accomplished. They knew the cards had not been tampered with because they were taken from the pack which Brian and Brenda played with most evenings.

After the card tricks, Meldrick, with Maci's help, made things disappear and reappear in obscure and impossible places. His small audience was mesmerised and clapped and asked for more. The magician and his assistant obliged and threw in a few jokes to keep the evening lively, thus creating much laughter and an enjoyable party atmosphere.

However, later when Anna went to her room she recalled the noise she felt she had heard the previous night and the horrible feeling that someone was in the room. She then remembered sensing that she had been watched while on the promenade a few days earlier and she suddenly felt very nervous. Furthermore, there was the mystery of the button she'd found that morning on the floor, the origin of which was still unexplained.

For comfort she switched on the television and selected a soothing music channel. She then prepared for bed but to ensure she had a good night's sleep, she stood a chair in front of the door so she that would know if it had been opened during the night and for extra measure, she sat Andy on the chair in the middle so she would know if he had moved. Feeling reassured that she was safe, and with calming music for comfort, she fell asleep soon after her head hit the pillow.

Chapter Eight

Anna woke on Saturday morning at seven o'clock. Having slept well and feeling refreshed, she climbed out of bed in a positive frame of mind.

Eager to get downstairs for breakfast, she skipped into the bathroom and took a quick shower, hopeful that Dominic and Josephina would be up so that she might learn how the ghost hunt had fared.

Once dressed she looked from the south facing window and out to the distant horizon where the sea twinkled in the morning sunlight beneath a sparse scattering of ominous grey clouds. She then glanced towards the smaller eastern window and smiled approvingly to where the sun's rays cast a long golden beam of light onto the cream coloured carpet. However, on averting her eyes, the smile quickly disappeared from her face. For on the window sill in the crystal glass vase were a dozen deep yellow roses.

Anna walked closer and touched the soft petals. Who could have put them there and were they there when she had gone to bed the previous evening? She thought it possible but unlikely. Alarmed at the prospect of someone having been in her room, she crossed to the door to check that the chair had not moved. It was in exactly the same place as she had positioned it and Andy had not moved from the middle of the seat where she had placed him. Anna checked both windows. They were firmly closed and latched.

As she brushed her hair she came to the conclusion that the unexplained appearance of the flowers must be trickery of some kind and there was only one person to whom that act could be attributed.

In the morning room, Meldrick and Maci were drinking coffee. They smiled as Anna entered the room.

"Good morning, young lady," said Meldrick, "I trust you slept well."

"Yes, I did, thank you," said Anna, returning a smile.

"Excellent."

"Okay," said Anna, placing both hands on her hips, "how did you do it?"

Meldrick frowned. "Do what?" he asked.

"The flowers," said Anna, wagging her finger. "I woke up this morning to find a dozen beautiful yellow roses in a vase on my window sill and I'm ninety nine point nine percent sure they weren't there last night."

Maci scowled and gave Meldrick a questioning look.

"I can assure you, Anna, that the roses have nothing to do with me. To be honest, I've never much been into flowers."

"I can vouch for that," said Maci, wistfully.

"But…but." Anna sat down at her table. "Where did they come from then?"

"Sounds like you have a secret admirer," said Brian, intrigued by the conversation, "and the fellow crept into your room in the dead of night as you slept."

"Oh, how romantic," said Maci, dreamily.

"But he couldn't have," said Anna, "because I put a chair in front of my door so that I'd know if it had been opened and I can assure you that it hadn't and Andy hadn't moved either."

"Who on earth is Andy?" asked Maci.

"A bear," said Anna, too shocked to explain.

Brenda looked alarmed. "Why would you put a chair in front of your door, dear? I mean, surely you don't feel unsafe here."

Anna sighed. "No, I don't. Well, yes, I do. That is to say, I don't feel unsafe. It's just that I keep getting the feeling that I'm being watched. Silly, I know and then one night I heard a strange noise and was convinced there was someone in my room."

"Oh dear, you poor girl," said Brenda, shocked, "I do hope that you're mistaken."

Anna looked downcast. "So do I, but now I feel even more freaked out than ever."

"I shouldn't let it worry you," said Brian, trying to reassure her, "I daresay when you ask around you'll most likely find the flowers were already in your room last night but because of a glass or two of wine you didn't even notice. I'm sure I wouldn't have done had we been in the same situation."

Anna smiled. "Yes, I expect you're right. It was probably even Poppy when she did my room yesterday because I told her the other day that I was very fond of yellow roses and there are some beauties in the gardens here."

"That's the right attitude," said Brenda, spreading a thick layer of ginger marmalade on a slice of toast. "Don't let things get you down, dear, because nothing's ever as bad as it first seems and there's always a simple explanation."

"No, you're right. I won't," said Anna, determined to adopt a positive attitude. She turned to Meldrick and Maci. "And I'm sorry for accusing you of playing tricks on me."

Meldrick chuckled. "Say no more, sweetheart, because I must admit your unfortunate predicament has given me an idea or two."

Maci giggled. "Surely not."

As Michelle entered the morning room from the kitchen, the vicar having eaten his breakfast, stood up and headed towards the other door. Anna frowned as he left the room, for during the conversation she and the other guests had conducted he had listened but not said a word. She had a sudden feeling of unease on realising the vicar's room was directly opposite hers. But then she smiled; how silly to suspect the poor vicar of any wrong doing just because he wasn't a chatterbox.

"I was hoping to see Dominic and Josephina during breakfast," said Maci, with a deep sigh, "as I'm longing to know how they got on last night."

"Me too," said Brenda, "they must have got back safely though because their car is out the back."

Brian shook his head. "I doubt you'll see them for an hour or two yet, I believe the ghost hunt wasn't due to wind up till four this morning and then they had to drive back here."

"Is the castle far from here?" Anna asked.

"No," said Michelle, clearing he vicar's table, "eight miles perhaps, ten miles at the most."

Later in the morning, having not seen her since the previous evening and knowing that when Poppy did arise, she would have the rooms to do, Anna went out into the gardens to read. As she sat down on a bench beneath a rose arbour, she noticed Josephina down by pond. Eager to hear how the ghost hunting had gone she walked across the lawn to join her.

"Lovely morning," said Anna, as she approached Josephina who was lying across the paving slabs on her stomach watching fish in the pond.

Josephina looked up. "For the time being, but I believe rain is forecast before lunchtime."

"Yes, I've noticed a grey cloud or two lurking above. I hope the day isn't going to be as wet as yesterday." She tilted her head to one side. "Do you mind if I join you?"

"No, not at all. I'm trying to count the fish but it's not very easy as they keep disappearing beneath the lily pads."

Anna sat down on the path. "I should think it's damn near impossible as they all look much the same anyway."

"Hmm, yes, they do and they keep moving. I should hate to be a fish. It must be incredibly boring and it'd be horrid to be wet all the time."

"There's no answer to that," said Anna, smothering a laugh.

Josephina rolled over and then sat up. "No, and it was a rather silly thing to say but I was just thinking out loud."

"Is Dominic not up yet?" Anna glanced up at the house.

Josephina shook her head. "No, the ghost hunt didn't finish till four and so it was getting on for five before we got back. I woke up an hour ago and then couldn't get back to sleep and so I got up."

"You must be starving because you've missed breakfast."

"No, actually I didn't. Michelle said to us yesterday that we must give her a shout when we got up and then she'd do us some toast and so that's what I did. Dominic will have to fend for himself though when he stirs but that probably won't be for an hour or two yet, and I put the 'Do not disturb' sign on the door as I left to remind Poppy we had a late night."

"I see, so how did the ghost hunt go? I'm dying to know. In fact we all are. It was one of the main topics of conversation during breakfast."

"Yes, I can imagine," said Josephina, her eyes sparkling. "It was brilliant, every minute of it, and the castle is such a spooky place. Although to be honest I didn't really see anything out of the ordinary but Dom did." She sighed. "He's really susceptible to such things and I suppose I'm not, but I wish I was."

"Oh, poor you," said Anna, sympathetically, "that must be so frustrating."

"It is, although I did hear a lot of strange noises including footsteps shuffling along a corridor. I sensed it when the temperature dropped as well without even looking at the thermometer."

"Oh, now that's creepy," said Anna, her imagination fired up, "So, what sort of things did Dominic see?"

"Orbs in all different of sizes and colours. I've picked them up with my camera before now but Dom can actually see them with the naked eye. Although I do question whether or not it might be possible that some of them are merely specks of dust on his glasses and I have to confess that might even be the case with the camera lens too."

"I've heard of ghostly orbs," said Anna, "but I didn't know that they came in different colours."

"Neither did I until I met Dominic. Apparently different colours mean different things but I can never remember what. All I know is an orb is the spirit of someone who has passed over. At least that's what the ghost hunters believe."

"Does that mean you have your doubts?"

Josephina paused before she answered. "Yes and no. I do believe there is something out there but at the same time a lot is just the imagination working overtime. I mean, if an individual or a group of people want and believe there to be ghosts in the places they are investigating, then it must be easy for them to imagine such presences are there. Especially when they're in an unknown territory surrounded by unfamiliar sounds and with very little or no lighting."

"And as you imply, with like-minded people," said Anna.

Josephina nodded. "Precisely."

Anna glanced up at the house and watched as the clouds passed over the tops of the three tall chimneys. "I think this place is fascinating and I love the chimneys. There is something eerie about them. They are the reason that I chose to come and stay here. Once I'd decided on Penzance, that is." She smiled. "That must sound really silly. I mean, who in their right mind would choose to stay somewhere because of the chimneys?"

Josephina nodded. "I know what you mean and I agree. Dom's fascinated by the house too but he says it's sad."

"Really, in what way?"

Josephina shrugged her shoulders. "Something about it having a sad past. He loves old buildings with a bit of character like this, and always seems able to sense if mysterious things might have happened. But don't be alarmed: he gets like that in lots of places he visits."

"I should imagine being with him is a bit spooky."

Josephina laughed. "It was at first but I'm used to his ways now."

"So did you come to Cornwall just because of the ghost hunt?"

"Yes, and it was a last minute decision. Dominic rang me last Saturday and out of the blue said that he wanted to go to Cornwall for a few days and could I get time off work. When I asked why the rush, he told me about the ghost hunt. He booked everything including our accommodation here and as you know we arrived on Monday."

"You were lucky to be able to get time off work at such short notice."

"Well, actually I'd already booked a couple of weeks off but he'd forgotten that."

"I see, so had you anything exciting planned for your time off?"

"Not really, I was going to decorate my flat, but this is much more fun."

"And the decorating can wait."

"Yes, it'll have to."

Anna noticed an engagement ring on Josephina's finger. "Have you and Dominic been together long?" she asked, keen to change the subject away from ghosts.

Josephina wrinkled her nose. "Umm, about two years, I think. We met in a churchyard of all places. I was putting flowers on my grandmother's grave and he was reading inscriptions."

"Reading inscriptions," repeated Anna, "Why was he doing that?"

"I think he was trying to establish the final resting place of someone or other. Something like that. I can't really remember as I was too fascinated by his presence to really take in what he said."

"So does he do anything other than hunt ghosts?"

Josephina smiled. "Oh yes, he's a surveyor."

Anna giggled. "How extraordinary. I'd never have guessed that in a hundred years. Oh, I'm sorry, I didn't mean to laugh, but it strikes me as comical, him being something down to earth like a surveyor and also a ghost hunter, the two just don't seem compatible."

"That's just what I said when I first met him but it doesn't seem so odd now."

"So what about you? Do you have a surprising occupation?"

"Not really," said Josephina, "well, actually, no not at all. I'm a florist."

"Oh, now that must be such a fascinating job. I love flowers, especially roses. In fact I love all flowers but the scented ones are my favourites."

As she spoke the sun disappeared behind a threatening black cloud and a few spots of rain fell from the heavens.

"Time to go in," said Anna, scrambling to her feet. Josephina did likewise.

Inside the house they met Maci in the hallway eager to hear news of the ghost hunt. And so Anna not wanting to intervene, excused herself and headed up the stairs to her room. On the landing, she met Poppy with a basket of white towels having just finished the last room. Anna promptly thanked her for the yellow roses.

Poppy looked nonplussed. "Roses. What roses?"

Anna's face dropped. "The dozen yellow roses in the vase on my window sill. Oh, please don't say you didn't put them there because Meldrick has already denied that it was one of his tricks."

Poppy shook her head. "I'm sorry, Anna, but I don't know what you're talking about."

"Come into my room and I'll show you."

Anna opened the door and they went inside. She pointed to the flowers and then sat down on the bed nearest the east window and dramatically rested her face in her hands.

"This morning I woke up to find these yellow roses on my window sill just as they are now and I was pretty sure they weren't here last night when I came to bed. Foolishly, I confronted Meldrick thinking he might be behind it. Daft, I know but I thought it might have been a magic trick. Needless to say, he said he wasn't. Brian suggested they must already have been here last night, which in retrospect seemed logical. I thought it was you, simply because I said the other day how much I liked yellow roses and of course you have access to the room. That does make sense, doesn't it?"

Poppy sat down on the other bed. "Yes, I can see where you're coming from but I don't know what to say, Anna, because it certainly wasn't me. Honestly."

Anna's face was devoid of colour. "But this is awful. I mean…Oh, my god, I feel sick."

Poppy tried to be positive. "I shouldn't worry, I expect they were from a secret admirer who just happens to wander around in the dead of night." She frowned, "But I can't think who he might be, unless it's the vicar."

Anna half-smiled. "Brian said that too. Not the possibility of it being the vicar, as amusing as I find the prospect is. I'm referring to the likelihood of it being a secret admirer. But that theory doesn't hold water because no-one could get in without a key, could they?"

"Not unless whoever it was, was good at picking locks." Poppy giggled. "Perhaps the vicar is really a burglar or better still an undercover police officer who is here to keep an eye on criminal activity in the area. I bet police officers know how to pick locks."

Anna shuddered and laughed at the same time. "Stop it, Poppy, you're scaring me. Anyway, no-one came in through my door because there was a chair in front of it last night and without doubt it did not move."

"A chair?" said Poppy, with a questioning scowl. "Why?"

"Because, well, the night before last I woke up in the early hours and heard a strange noise. I also felt that there was someone in the room, but when I switched the light on there was no-one here…thank goodness. All the same, last night I put the chair in front of the door to prove to myself that I was being silly. I even sat Andy on the chair, and this morning the chair hadn't moved, nor had Andy. Yet the flowers were here just as you see them now. It just doesn't make sense."

Poppy stood up. "Well, I don't know what to say unless it was one of Meldrick's tricks. I mean, they were pretty convincing, weren't they? And I've no idea how he did any of the ones we saw last night."

Anna's eyes widened. "No, neither have I, unless he really can do magic."

"Do you believe in ghosts?" Maci asked Meldrick as they walked arm in arm along the Mousehole harbour wall in-between showers.

"I'm not really sure about that. I love the notion of ghosts and the fact that I might even go on to be one at the end of my days, but if they do exist, I wonder why they keep themselves to themselves so much, because apart from Dominic I don't think I've ever come across anyone that has seen one." He chuckled, "No-one with a ha'p'orth of sense, anyway."

"I'm inclined to agree and I get the impression that even Jo is rather sceptical and considers some of Dominic's claims to be dubious."

"Is that right?"

"Yes, she told me when I asked her about last night's ghost hunt."

"Oh, I didn't know you'd seen her today."

"Hmm, I did. I bumped into her in the hallway when I went down to the morning room to get my phone which I'd left on the table. She'd just come in from the garden because it had started to rain."

"Well, whatever we think we must not pour scorn on Dominic's assertions, my dear, Maci, for if we do he may declare that there is no such thing as magic."

Maci laughed. "And that would never do."

Chapter Nine

Later in the day the rain showers cleared and Poppy asked Anna if she would like to go with her to take Rafe for a walk. It was a chore that her parents usually shared by taking it in turns but as James was in the throes of lifting the floor tiles in the old scullery along with Alfie, and Michelle needed to go shopping, they asked Poppy if she'd take him out instead. Anna readily agreed to the walk and so the three of them left The Old Tile House around three o'clock and headed for the coastal path which ran between the railway tracks and the beach, but to make a change, Poppy suggested they take a different route from when they had previously gone down to the coast.

The pavements were still wet following the scattering of showers earlier in the day and a formation of grey clouds threatened further rain still. A light wind was blowing from the north east hence the day felt cool and the girls both wore jackets and carried umbrellas.

As they walked along a quiet leafy road chatting about the band they were going to see in Pentrillick that evening, they came across a detached pebble-dashed bungalow, painted white. Anna slowed as they passed by its gate and then paused to peek over the low garden wall where a vast array of colourful flowers bloomed in beds and long borders. Poppy folded her arms and mocked boredom as Anna extolled the beauty of the cottage garden, but Anna's enthusiasm could not be dampened especially when she saw a wooden plaque fixed to the wall beside the front door. The name of the house was Greenwood.

"Now, if I had pots of money," said Anna, delighted by the choice of house name, "I'd buy that bungalow and live in it. Just me, Andy and a dog of some sort."

Poppy giggled. "What, even though it's not for sale?"

"Well, yes, that would be a slight obstacle, I suppose, but as I don't have any money anyway it's not really a problem. It's nice to dream though, don't you think?"

They resumed their walk.

"Hmm, yes, but as regards that house being right for you I think it might look a bit odd if your address was Miss Anna Greenwood, Greenwood, Hillcrest Avenue, Penzance, Cornwall."

Anna scowled. "Oh, I hadn't thought of that. Anyway, it's not going to happen, is it?"

"Sadly, I very much doubt it."

"So, where do you think your dream house would be, Poppy?"

"I don't really know. I might have to have more than one. You know, a house in the country for the summer and a pied-à-terre in the winter. And then of course it would be nice to have a villa somewhere on foreign shores."

"I've never been abroad and I daresay that I never shall. I can't speak any foreign languages anyway, although as I said the other day I did learn French at school, but I was pretty rubbish." She laughed, "Pierre can vouch for that. It's silly, but for some reason learning a foreign language never really appealed back then which is a shame as it might be useful one day, but I doubt it. I'm too much of a home-bird. Well, a home-country bird to be more precise because I definitely think I could live in Cornwall even though I've lived all my life in the City."

"Don't be such a pessimist, Anna. You have your whole life ahead of you and so who knows what it might hold. The world is your oyster."

"Maybe, but my aspirations are very humble compared with yours, and always will be because I can't see how I could ever achieve greatness even if I'd want to."

Poppy sighed. "Many would see that as a virtue, Anna. Your modesty, I mean. And I suppose if I'm honest I've always been rather spoiled. I like the fact you're down to earth and you don't want the top brick off the chimney. It's a refreshing change, so on reflection, please stay just the way you are."

When they arrived at the beach, Poppy let Rafe off his lead and the two girls followed him across the wet sand. Anna, not having been to the beach since she had encountered the mysterious set of footprints, repeatedly looked over her shoulder to make sure that the same thing was not happening again. To her relief their prints were without escort. She smiled to herself and conceded her overreaction earlier in the week had been very silly indeed.

In the evening, Anna met up with Poppy and Alfie for the prearranged trip to Pentrillick to see the local band, Pebbles and Sand. It was drizzling when they left The Old Tile House but to the relief of the girls there was very little wind to ruffle their carefully styled hair.

James drove them to the Crown and Anchor but they said not to worry about picking them up as they would get a taxi home.

The band were already playing when they walked into the pub and every table was taken. Alfie, who had arranged to meet his friend, Baz who lived in the village, attempted to find him but because of the crowd he had to text him to establish his whereabouts. When they finally tracked him down, Alfie quickly introduced Baz to the girls in between numbers played by the band, after which they bought drinks and joined others already enjoying the performance.

During the interval they refilled their glasses and went out onto the terrace for a breath of fresh air. Because of the light drizzle earlier in the evening the seating outside was still wet and so everyone on the terrace was standing. Baz, they discovered was also a gardener and it was through a garden centre that he and Alfie knew each other.

As they were all chatting someone called Alfie's name. He waved as two people squeezed through the crowd to join them.

"Poppy, Anna, this is my big sister, Chloe," Alfie said as he kissed her on the cheek, "and this chap is Colin, her husband. And Chloe and Colin, these lovely ladies are Poppy, the boss's daughter and Anna who is staying at The Old Tile House."

They all shook hands.

"Louise told me you called into the café the other day," said Chloe, "but I was out. I'm sorry to have missed you. Was that the first time you'd been to the village?"

Poppy nodded. "Yes, Alfie has been extolling its virtues for ages so when Anna arrived in Cornwall last weekend, I at last had someone to come here with."

"Oh, poor Billy-no-mates," said Alfie, unsympathetically.

Poppy nudged him in the ribs. "You've changed your tune. I was a lovely lady a few minutes ago."

"Yes, but ninety nine point nine percent of that compliment was directed at Anna because she knows how to behave."

Rather than rise to his bait, Poppy ignored him and instead addressed Chloe. "Have you had the café long?" she asked.

"About three years. I wanted to have my own business and so because Colin grew up in Pentrillick we thought it would be the ideal place to have one. The café was already established when we bought it but the previous owner sold because she wasn't in the best of health and it was getting too much for her."

"And it's a little gold mine in the summer, isn't it, Chloe?" Alfie said.

"Yes, in the summer, but as with all businesses you have to look at income over the year and sometimes in the winter we're very quiet."

"So are you are able to keep on that nice lady we met the other day, all the year round?" Anna asked.

"Oh yes," said Chloe, "I wouldn't be without my nice lady, she's a treasure, isn't she, Baz?"

Baz pulled a funny face. "Yeah, she's alright."

"Louise is Baz's mum," said Alfie, seeing the confused looks on Poppy's and Anna's faces.

Colin laughed. "Lots of people in these Cornish villages are related so it always pays to be careful what you say about others when talking to strangers."

Anna smiled. "Well, I'm staying in Penzance and will only be here for another week but I'll bear that in mind for future reference."

"And I'm back at uni in a week or so," said Poppy, "but to avoid any future blunders, I shall store that piece of information in the old grey matter."

When the band began to play again they returned indoors and saw that several people had begun to dance and so they joined them. The evening was going well; the atmosphere was joyous and the band were extremely talented.

Anna deemed the occasion was nearing perfection as she watched coloured lights flash over the band and their musical instruments, across the dancers and then the onlookers standing close by.

Singing along quietly to herself during a slower number of which she was very fond, she dreamily glanced into the crowd. Her jaw dropped and she gasped as the words of the song froze on her lips and her feet stopped dancing. For standing behind a girl with long blonde hair, was the man from the train. Anna held out her hand determined to point him out to Poppy, but Poppy was out of reach and when she looked again, the man had moved towards the bar. Not wanting to lose sight of him, she slipped into the crowd just in time to see him go out of the front door. She followed, but as she stepped onto the pavement there was no-one there. She looked both ways and then walked round to the car park, but the only people there were two girls sitting on a bench in the smoker's shelter giggling over something on one of their mobile phones. She walked past them and down to the far end of the car park. The light from pub's terrace shone down onto the beach and highlighted the white frothy waves as they tumbled onto the shore, but no-one was there.

Anna walked back out to the street and again looked in both directions. Suddenly she heard footsteps approaching. She leaned back against the wall of the pub as someone appeared from a narrow lane on the other side of the road. Her heart sank as in the light from a street lamp she saw the figure of a middle aged man with a big bushy beard. He crossed the road and nodded to her as he passed by and went into the pub. Anna sighed. Once again the man from the train had vanished without trace.

Chapter Ten

Anna woke very early on Sunday morning just as day was beginning to break. Feeling thirsty, she slipped out of bed, went into the bathroom and drank a glass of water. On glancing in the mirror, she tutted to see that she had not removed the previous night's make-up, a routine of which she was usually very fussy. Determined that it must be removed before she returned to bed, she reached for her bag of cosmetics and thoroughly cleansed her face. However, once the task was completed she realised that the process had rendered her wide awake. Seeing little point then in going back to bed, she crossed over to the south facing window to view the morning after first checking that no more roses had appeared on the east facing window sill.

Kneeling on the cushioned window seat she rested her elbows on the ledge and looked out to the distant horizon where a light mist lingered over the sea and part-shrouded St Michael's Mount. Wondering if it might be spreading inland she glanced down to the gardens below and was relieved to see that visibility there was relatively clear. But then something caught her eye. She squinted and blinked, sure that she had seen movement amongst the shrubbery alongside the driveway. She rubbed her eyes and tried to adjust her vision to the dim morning light, and then she frowned. Without doubt someone was down there. She could see the outline of a dark figure crouched and part-hidden amongst the branches of a fuchsia bush. Suddenly another figure appeared from behind the hydrangeas on the other side of the driveway. Again the figure was crouched and wearing dark clothes. Anna was alarmed and unsure what to do. She was certain no-one would be up and so there was no-one she could speak to. She paced the room trying to think and then again looked from the window. To her horror a third figure was creeping across the lawn towards the house. Stifling a scream she ran from the room, across the landing and down the adjacent passage to Poppy's room. She didn't knock on the door but burst straight in and shook Poppy with both of her hands. Poppy woke and instantly cursed.

"What the hell are you doing, Anna?"

"I'm sorry," said Anna, close to tears, "but from my window I can see there are people in the garden. At least three of them and they're behaving very suspiciously. Come and see because I'm afraid they're going to break in."

Poppy leapt from her bed and dashed into Anna's room. There were now four dark figures creeping across the lawn.

"What the...." Poppy ran from the room shouting for her parents on the floor above, leaving Anna standing on the landing shivering with fear.

Suddenly there was a loud crash from down below. Someone was hammering on the front door.

"Open up...police," shouted a deep voice.

James and Michelle appeared on the stairs wearing dressing gowns and both ran down to the hallway. Poppy followed but Anna remained on the landing too afraid to move.

James opened the front door and four police officers rushed in.

"Do you know this man?" asked the first officer showing James and Michelle a photograph along with his identification.

James frowned. "Why, yes, it looks like the vicar but without any hair."

"Vicar, my foot. Where is he?"

"Upstairs, first floor, the only door on the left," said Michelle, part-hiding behind her husband.

"Thank you."

Brenda and Brian Cooke emerged from their room at the same time that Dominic and Josephina appeared on the stairs from their room on the upper floor, closely followed by Meldrick and Maci.

"What's all the racket about?" Brian asked.

"I don't really know," said Anna, in earnest.

As all four officers ran up the stairs, the door of the vicar's room was noisily flung open and Roger Mitchell ran out zipping up his trousers and with shoes tucked beneath his arm. Anna gasped and ducked back inside her doorway as the vicar stumbled across the landing towards the window. With one hand he yanked back the voile curtain and with little effort pulled up the sash window and threw out his shoes. He then began to climb over the sill, but he wasn't quick enough and two of the officers grabbed him before his second foot had left the floor. Anna felt the colour drain from her face as they roughly pulled the vicar back onto the landing. A struggle ensued as the officers tried to snap handcuffs around the vicar's wrists and in the scuffle his mop of thick, dark hair fell onto the floor revealing a glistening bald head with a giant menacing eye tattooed on its crown.

Everyone was down promptly for breakfast and the room buzzed with excited chatter. Through Michelle and James they had learned that Roger Mitchell wasn't a vicar at all. In fact he wasn't even Roger Mitchell. His real name was Shane Scully and he was on the run after escaping from prison where he was serving a long sentence for armed robbery.

"Well, who'd have thought it?" said Brenda, absentmindedly stirring twice the amount of sugar into her tea as she usually took, "he seemed such a nice young man too, even though he seldom spoke to anyone."

Brian frowned and muttered, "That's hardly surprising under the circumstances, is it? Not having much to say, I mean."

"I'm surprised I knew nothing about the man," said Meldrick, "I like to keep up with the news but the fact that there was an escaped prisoner on the run somehow passed me by."

"Same here," said Brian, "although according to James he's been on the run for a couple of months so I might have read about it back then but have since forgotten. That's the trouble with the Internet, we get such a lot of news these days that not much of it sticks."

Brenda looked at the table where Shane Scully normally sat. "And it didn't help that his behaviour was perfectly normal."

"Hmm, well I think one of us might have smelled a rat had he behaved liked a crook," said Josephina, with a laugh.

"True," agreed Brenda.

"And, my dear, Josephina," said Dominic, his brows knitted, "may I ask just how you think a criminal might behave? I mean, surely even the most brutal of men must at times be kind-hearted and courteous to his fellow men."

"Do you really think so?" Brenda asked.

Dominic nodded. "Absolutely. Remember the old saying: *There is so much good in the worst of us, and so much bad in the best of us, that it ill behoves any of us to find fault with the rest of us.*"

"Never a truer word," said Meldrick, slapping his hand on the table top, "or should I say words?"

"That's so sad," said Maci, "I thought he was really cute because once or twice he winked at me."

"Oh, he did, did he?" Chuckled Meldrick, "well, he won't be doing that again."

Brian suddenly laughed. "And when all is said and done, you've got to hand it to old Shane, because it was a damn good disguise."

"Too good," said Brenda, scowling as she took a sip of her over-sweet tea, "I'm not sure that I'll ever be able to trust a vicar again."

After breakfast, Brenda ventured out in the rain to post a birthday card to her sister in Liverpool. The morning felt chilly and so she hurried along beneath her umbrella, cautiously avoiding sporadic puddles on the wet pavement.

When she arrived back at The Old Tile House, Brian was not in their room and as he had the key, she couldn't get in. Knowing he would not be out in the garden she went back downstairs to look for him. As she passed the door of the guests' lounge she heard Dominic inside chatting to someone. On the off-chance it might be Brian to whom he was speaking, she opened the door and peeped inside. To her surprise, Dominic was in there alone.

"Oh, hmm, have you by any chance seen Brian since breakfast?" she asked, looking behind the door.

Dominic shook his head. "No, sorry. Can't help you there."

"Oh, well, never mind, thank you, I'll try elsewhere." She closed the door but as she walked away she again heard Dominic speaking. The hairs on the back of her neck stood up. Who was Dominic talking too? As she moved away from the door she suddenly felt uneasy. Either Dominic was talking to himself or there was a presence in the house that only he, being a ghost hunter, was aware of. She shuddered. Perhaps Anna's roses weren't left by a secret admirer at all. At least, not one that was living.

Brenda found Brian in the morning room talking to James about tennis and the US Open men's final due to take place the following day.

"Back already?" said Brian, as she walked into the room. "Sorry, love, I didn't think you'd be that quick or I'd have given you the key before you left."

"That's okay, I wasn't gone long because there was a post box at the end of the road." She looked quizzically at James. "Please don't think me batty, James, but I think Dominic might be right and your house really is haunted?"

James threw back his head and laughed. "Now why might you think that? Surely you've not been accosted by an apparition."

"No, no, nothing like that. But when I was looking for Brian just now, without doubt I heard Dominic talking to someone in the lounge. Thinking it might be Brian, I looked in there and saw that Dominic was on his own. Needless to say, I didn't stay but as I closed the door and walked away I heard him talking again."

James chuckled again. "And so you think he might have been talking to the spirit of someone who has passed into the unknown?"

"Well, yes it makes sense, don't you think?"

"Makes sense, you numpty," said Brian, giving her arm a friendly tap, "Come on, Brenda. I expect the poor bloke was talking to someone on his mobile." He tutted and then laughed. "Ghost indeed."

Anna and Poppy met up in the afternoon and as the rain had stopped they agreed it would be nice to take a walk down to the sea front to get a bit of fresh air and exercise before the next lot of rain arrived. To be on the safe side, Poppy said that she would fetch the umbrellas, and while she was gone, Anna went up to her room to get her jacket from the wardrobe.

Five minutes later, Poppy, wearing her coat and with the umbrellas dangling from her wrist, sat at the foot of the stairs waiting for Anna. Ten minutes passed by and still Poppy was alone and waiting. To pass the time, she checked her phone to see if there were any messages from her uni friends. As she returned the phone to her pocket, she saw that yet a further ten minutes had passed and there was still no sign of Anna. She stood up anxious to discover what could possibly be keeping her friend.

On the upstairs landing, Poppy tapped on Anna's door and called her name. After a few minutes the door slowly opened.

"Are you okay?" Poppy asked, on seeing a look of bewilderment on Anna's face, "You look confused. Is anything wrong?"

Anna took Poppy by the arm and pulled her into the room. "Come on and I'll show you."

Inside the room she released her grip on Poppy's arm and pointed to the built-in wardrobe.

"I'm still trying to fathom things out. The thing is, I opened the wardrobe doors to get my coat and as I pulled it from the hanger the pocket caught on a coat hook on the back panel." Anna opened the wardrobe doors and pointed to the hook in question.

"Hmm, yes, I knew that was there. Mum reckons it is for belts or something like that, but what of it?"

"Well, when I freed my coat I felt sure the hook shifted a bit and so I don't really know why, but I gave it a pull and then a push but nothing moved. You try."

Poppy unenthusiastically did as she was asked and nothing happened. "I can't see what you're getting at, Anna."

"Now push it to the left. You have to do it really hard because it's heavy and takes quite a bit of effort."

Poppy obliged and to her amazement she was able to move the whole centre back panel of the wardrobe to one side. Behind it was a large void.

"But...what?" Poppy muttered, "I don't understand."

"Now step through the gap," said Anna, pulling aside some of her garments hanging on the rail, "and then push against the panel in front of you."

"I'm not sure that I want to," said Poppy. "I feel nervous which is silly."

"Go on," said Anna, "I promise that you'll come to no harm."

Poppy stepped through the gap and jumped when her head hit something and caused it to rattle.

"It's just empty coat hangers," said Anna, "carry on through."

Poppy took another step and pushed against the panel in front of her. As it flung open, she realised she was standing in another wardrobe and when she peeped around the door she found herself looking into the unoccupied family guest room. In a daze she stepped out onto the carpet. Anna followed.

"See," said Anna, "there's a coat hook on this side of the back panel too, and so each room is accessible from the other. Rather clever, don't you think?"

"Well, yes, but how come neither of my parents know of this? Alfie too for that matter. Wait here, Anna, I must go and find them."

Michelle and James were as intrigued as Anna and Poppy.

"Well, I never," said James, stepping back and forth between the two wardrobes, "What a brilliant find, Anna. Clever girl."

"Isn't it?" said Anna, feeling smug, "and it's so subtly hidden."

James stepped back away from the wardrobe in the family room and sat down on the double bed. "To be honest we never looked at any of the guest rooms very thoroughly when we moved here simply because they were in excellent decorative order. Had we needed to give the wardrobes a coat of paint then we might have noticed the hooks moved when we were doing it."

"I doubt it," said Michelle, sitting down beside her husband, "because we wouldn't have painted the insides. I wonder how long ago they were built."

"Good point," said James. He stood up and then ran his hands over the inside panel. "The back here looks quite old, and so I should imagine it was a hundred years or so ago. These definitely aren't the original doors though so I reckon they've been changed quite recently. Probably even by the plumber chap we bought the house from."

"I wonder why they made the secret doorway though," said Poppy. "I mean what purpose would it serve?"

"Don't know," chuckled James, "but it would have been handy for a bit of hanky-panky."

Michelle giggled. "Trust you to come up with that."

"Anyway," said Anna, "whatever the reason, I'm very grateful to whoever it was that designed or built it because at least now I have an explanation as to how someone got into my room and put the roses on my window sill."

"Oh, yes, Poppy was telling us about that the other day," said Michelle, "I wonder who it was."

"More to the point, which roses are they?" said James, "That's assuming they came from our garden." They all went back into Anna's room and James sniffed the flowers on the window sill. "Ah, the old ones," he said, "Reliable old Arthur Bell. Someone has good taste."

Poppy frowned. "Never mind about the name of the roses, I'm more concerned about the secret door. I mean, who could have known about it? It's news to us and we live here. It makes no sense at all."

Chapter Eleven

Anna woke in the middle of the night to find her room partly lit by fading moonlight. Hoping that no intruders had crept in through the back of the wardrobe while she had been sleeping, she slowly peeped over the top of the bedclothes and cast her eyes around the room. All was quiet in the house and everything looked as it should until she saw the other bed. Slowly she sat up. Surely someone was lying there beneath the white duvet? Her heart began to race as she silently pushed back her bedclothes and slipped her feet out onto the floor. Quietly, so as not to disturb the sleeping intruder, she then tip-toed across the room. But as she approached the spare bed she heaved a great sigh of relief, for no-one was there. It was an illusion: a shadow cast by Anna's clothes hanging on the back of a chair where they obstructed the moonlight.

Giggling over the unnecessary action that her overactive imagination had caused, she jumped back into her own bed and picked up Andy the bear. "I think I'm on the verge of insanity, my dear friend," she said, as she snuggled back down beneath the bedclothes, "I see spooks in every corner now."

Feeling reassured, she fell asleep almost instantly and slept peacefully for a further five hours.

After breakfast, Anna took her Kindle outside to read but because there was a fresh wind blowing across the lawn she went into the summer house for shelter so that she could finish the book she had started to read on the train.

It was warm and bright in the little wooden house for the sun had been shining in through its many windows since it had first risen several hours earlier. But Anna knew the warmth was unlikely to continue for rain was forecast and already grey clouds were gathering further west.

With all the seating to choose from, Anna sat down on a small two seater sofa. She then kicked off her shoes and tucked up her feet beside her on the cushions.

It took less than an hour for Anna to finish her book and knowing that Poppy wouldn't be out for a while as nearly all of the guest rooms were occupied, she laid her head on the back of the sofa and closed her eyes. Before she knew it she was fast asleep, dreaming, and watching her hands skip along the keyboard of an upright piano which stood in a dimly lit corner beside an exposed stone wall. Around the piano, its case as black as ebony, stood her fellow guests at The Old Tile House excitedly watching as she played and heartily sang. And when she finished her recital and took a bow, they clapped with such enthusiasm that the hair on the head of each guest fell to the floor. In her dream Anna laughed, flattered by the rapturous applause, and when she reached for the piano lid to close it, she saw that three keys in a row were chipped thus causing her to check that the nail varnish on her fingers was not damaged. A sudden loud click was followed by the sound of repetitive clonks like footsteps on wooden boards and she saw the vicar running across the beach leaving footprints in the sand.

A sudden laugh caused her quickly to open her eyes and see Alfie had taken a seat on a chair opposite. On the table beside him, he'd laid down a plate on which sat a teacake and in his hands he held a mug of steaming coffee.

"You were fast asleep then, lazy bones," he said, breaking a piece off the teacake, "and dreaming too I reckon by the scowl on your face."

Anna stifled a yawn. "Oh no, I hate it when I have a nap during the day because it makes it more difficult to sleep at night."

"Same with me," he agreed, "You'd better go for a five mile run to tire yourself out."

"Ugh, I hate running but couldn't go anyway because it's going to rain."

"Just starting," said Alfie, "well, drizzling."

Anna sat up straight. "Was I really scowling?"

Alfie nodded. "Yep, and singing too before that. I could hear you as I approached the summer house."

Anna looked alarmed. "Oh no, I don't have a very good singing voice. I hope it wasn't too awful."

"Suited me fine," said Alfie, with a grin, "because it scared off next door's cat which was asleep on the veranda of the summer house."

Anna laughed. "I take it you're not very fond of cats."

"They're alright but I like to feed the birds and it's not possible with Henry being a frequent visitor."

"Henry, so is Henry the black cat I've seen around?"

"Yes, as black as soot."

"Ah, so, when I heard the lady next door calling Henry the other day she wasn't talking to her husband or brother at all. It was her cat."

Alfie nodded. "That's right. Martha's cat is called Henry and her husband is Albert."

"Oh dear, silly me, but I must admit I rather like the name Henry for a cat."

Alfie grinned. "I do too. Apparently, according to James who gets on well with the neighbours, he's called Henry because he's the eighth cat they've had."

Anna laughed. "I like that, but I'm surprised Henry dare come over here at all with Rafe charging around. Henry that is, not the neighbour."

"Rafe's as daft as a brush and likes Henry's company. I must admit he's been behaving a bit odd lately though. Rafe that is, not Henry. I reckon it's something to do with that ghost chap and Rafe can see something us lesser mortals can't."

Anna instinctively looked over her shoulder. "What...what sort of things do you mean?"

"Who knows?" said Alfie, "but I've seen him bark and growl and stare at spots where there's clearly nothing there and I'd never seen him do that before. The first time I noticed it would have been around the time that Dominic arrived."

On Monday afternoon new guests arrived at The Old Tile House. Anna learned of this from Brenda whom she met on the stairs after leaving her room where she had been to change prior to going out with Poppy and Josephina.

"From what I've gathered they sound rather posh," said Brenda, glancing over her shoulder to check that the coast was clear,

"They're called Margot and Hugo, you see. Of course, had it been me instead of Brian who bumped into them earlier then I would have found out more." She tutted. "Such a shame but I'm afraid Brian's not very good at extracting information from people, especially when he's on holiday."

Anna smiled. "Well I daresay you'll have ample opportunity to learn more in the next few days. That's if they're here for more than one night."

"Yes, dear, I certainly hope so. Unfortunately Brian wasn't even able to establish that. The length of their visit I mean. All I know is they're in the family room because that's where Brian saw them coming out from, but there are only the two of them. No children or anything like that."

"Oh, they're my next door neighbours then," said Anna, thinking of the secret door behind the wardrobe.

"Yes, of course, that hadn't registered with me. Anyway, I'm sure at breakfast tomorrow I'll get the opportunity to suss them out or you might even beat me to it."

Anna moved forwards ready to continue down the stairs. "Perhaps you'll see them later if they go down to the guests' lounge."

Brenda sighed thoughtfully. "Hmm, trouble is we won't be there. We're going out tonight to the cinema, but I'll make sure I take a peek in there when we get back. Just in case." She rubbed her hands together gleefully. "I do love it when we get new guests. Anyway, I'm holding you up which is very thoughtless of me. So off you go, dear."

"Okay, bye Brenda."

"Goodbye dear."

Anna, Poppy and Josephina spent the afternoon dodging showers and trawling the shops until the very last one closed. They then went into a pub for a quick drink and a bite to eat. It was their intention to be back at The Old Tile House within the hour of entering the pub, but the time seemed to go quickly and they enjoyed each other's company. Before they knew it, it was nearly nine o'clock.

"I must go," said Josephina, on realising the time. "Dominic will have been back for ages and no doubt wondering where I am."

"Where did you say he had gone again?" Anna asked, feeling slightly light-headed.

"I'm not really sure because I was planning what I'd like to buy when he was telling me and so I wasn't actually listening but I think it might have been something to do with Friday's ghost hunt." She giggled. "On the other hand it probably wasn't."

"Well," said Poppy, "wherever he's been he can't be too worried about you or he would have rung by now, wouldn't he? Look to see if you've had a text or a missed call."

Josephina pulled her mobile phone from her handbag and then giggled. "He can't leave me a message or ring me because he doesn't have a mobile phone."

"Really?" said Anna.

"Why ever not?" said Poppy. "I thought everyone had one these days. All of my grandparents do and so does my great granny and she's in her nineties."

Josephina dropped the phone back into her handbag. "Dominic is a bit old fashioned and doesn't like them. He also says he doesn't want one in case it should ring at an inopportune moment."

"Like when he's ghost hunting?" said Anna.

"Precisely."

Anna drained her wine glass. "Why? Is it because it might interfere with ghostly signals or something like that?"

Josephina wrinkled her nose. "Yes, I suppose so."

"But that's silly," said Poppy, "because he could always switch it off, if and when he didn't want to be disturbed. That's what most people do."

"I know, but he's very obstinate and set in his ways."

"I used to think your Dominic was really creepy," said Anna, "Well, actually I still do but not as much as I did."

"Yes, I know what you mean but it's just the way he comes across," said Josephina. "In reality he's very sensitive. Caring too. Bless him."

"But does he really see ghosts?" Poppy asked, with a scowl, "I have to confess that I'm very sceptical about people who make such claims."

Josephina nodded slowly. "Yes, I'm sure that he does. He's very earnest and I don't think he would make things up."

"So where's your next ghost hunt?" Anna asked.

"Goodness knows, there probably won't be one for a while. I think this one has quite drained Dominic, that and the fact that The Old Tile House saddens him."

Poppy looked alarmed. "The Old Tile House saddens him. Why?"

"He claims something horrible once happened there but he either won't or can't elaborate," Josephina paused and ran her fingers slowly around the rim of her glass, "It's weird, but I get the feeling it's something to do with the driveway. He never speaks when we walk down it. His manner is always one of reverence and his eyes dart around seemingly full of sorrow."

"That's creepy," said Anna.

"He's having you on," said Poppy.

Josephina shook her head. "I don't think so. On the other hand perhaps he is. Who knows? He certainly has an interest in amateur dramatics."

"Well, there you are," said Poppy, drinking the last drop of lager from her pint glass, "it's all a bit of an act."

"Hmm, I think I'd like to go along with that theory too," said Anna.

"Anyway, if you can't get in touch with Dominic, Jo, and he can't get in touch with you, then I suggest we have another drink," said Poppy, rising unsteadily to her feet and picking up their empty glasses. "Same again, girls?"

"Yes, please," answered Anna and Josephina in unison.

It was another hour before they left the pub and by then all three were feeling hungry again.

"I think I'm going to get a pizza," said Poppy, "I can pick one up on the way home."

Josephina agreed. "Good idea. I'll join you in the queue."

Anna groaned. "I ought to do the same but I hate eating late, especially cheese, it gives me nightmares."

"Perhaps you'll have a nice nightmare about your lovely train man," said Poppy, swerving to miss walking into a lamppost.

Anna nodded thoughtfully. "Hmm, but is there such a thing as a nice nightmare?"

"Don't know," said Poppy, "but if you have a pizza you might find out."

Dominic was in the guests' lounge talking to Meldrick and Maci when they arrived back at The Old Tile House. He took one look at the state of the three girls and laughed.

"I take it you've had a good day and evening," he said.

"Brilliant," said Josephina, sitting down heavily by his side, "have you had a good day too?"

"Yes, thank you." He looked at Poppy and Anna swaying in the doorway. "I think you two had better sit down too before you fall down."

Anna and Poppy sat down at the table opposite each other and opened up their pizza boxes.

"Would anyone like a piece?" Anna asked, waving a slice of pizza.

Meldrick, Maci and Dominic all declined her offer and so she ate it all herself.

It was just after eleven when Anna went up to her room. She cleaned her teeth but was too tired to remove her make-up and fell asleep with Andy in her arms the minute her head hit the pillow.

As feared, she dreamed, but the dream was not a nightmare nor was it nice but it did involve the mysterious man from the train. He was standing beside the pond in the gardens of The Old Tile House with the white moon beaming down onto his tall, dark figure. On the surface of the still water, his reflection shimmered gently beside the golden yellow water lily flowers and its fleshy green leaves.

On top of the summer house roof, Henry the cat watched as the mysterious man looked up towards Anna who was standing on the front door steps. He beckoned her to join him and merrily she skipped barefooted across the lawn to his side, but when she looked into the pond, she saw that she had no reflection.

Behind them the house loomed dark and sinister and the moonlight caused each of its three tall chimneys to cast eerie shadows across its long tiled roof. High above, millions of stars twinkled in the clear, dark sky and the only sound was the wind rustling the leaves of the weeping willow tree.

The man from the train reached out and took Anna's hand and then together they slowly rose up and away from the ground and over the roof of The Old Tile House and the surrounding houses. Anna's long nightdress flapped and fluttered around her bare legs and the gentle breeze tousled her long brown hair. As The Old Tile House disappeared into the night, they drifted over the winding streets of Penzance and row upon row of houses.

In the distance far behind, the calm sea sparkled in the moonlight and St Michael's Mount loomed high on the horizon. Eventually, they gently floated down and stepped onto damp grass beneath a tall, horse chestnut tree. As Anna regained her balance she glanced around and saw that they were in a sleepy burial ground.

The mysterious man released Anna's hand and his eyes turned to gaze, mesmerised, onto a patch of matted grass. Upon it stood a granite urn containing yellow roses and above towered a polished, granite headstone. He turned away and Anna followed him along a gravel path. Beside a laurel bush, loose earth was heaped upon a canvas sheet lying on the freshly mown grass and the deep hole from which it was taken, was covered with old weather-beaten wooden boards. The mysterious man knelt down and carefully pushed the boards to one side. He then stared, his face expressionless, into the deep, dark hole that was to be the final resting place of someone recently deceased.

Clutching her long nightdress, Anna knelt down beside him and she too looked into the pitch-black grave. As she stared, the darkness before her began to gyrate, each whirl distorted her vision and as they rotated and quickened she felt giddy and light-headed. Afraid that she might fall, she outstretched her hand for something to steady her balance but the man from the train was no longer there, and with nothing to grasp, she felt herself falling into the bleak, black abyss.

Instantly, Anna woke up; her whole body was bathed in perspiration and a feeling of suffocation was causing her to gasp for breath. She sat up and wiped her forehead on the back of her hand.

The room was in semi darkness and as she slid from her bed, Andy dropped onto the floor. Shivering, Anna crossed to the window and looked down onto the garden below. The faded moon was shining onto the pond as in her dream, but Henry the cat was not on the summer house roof and to her relief the lawn was devoid of any presence. Shakily, she picked up Andy and climbed back into bed, but sleep evaded her and she lay awake for several, long hours.

Chapter Twelve

Tuesday morning brought forth a fine, sunny day and just before eight, Anna dragged herself from her bed, bleary eyed and listless. Still disturbed by the clarity of her dream and tired through lack of sleep, she removed her make-up and then took a shower to help wake herself up.

In the morning room she realised she had very little appetite for breakfast but managed to force down a cup of tea and a slice of toast to keep up her strength.

As she finished her toast two unfamiliar people entered the morning room. Anna assumed they were the new guests, Margot and Hugo and her assumption was ratified when Brian addressed them thus.

"Are you alright, Anna?" Josephina asked, "I must say you look a bit peaky."

Anna half-smiled. "I said eating late and especially cheese would give me nightmares and it did. Well, to be fair not nightmares but I certainly dreamed and then I lay awake for ages unable to get back to sleep."

"Oh no, poor you. I slept like a top and didn't dream at all," said Josephina.

"And you snored," said Dominic, "most unladylike."

"I didn't," said Josephina, crossly, "did I?"

Dominic nodded. "Yes, my dear, you did. But don't worry, it's quite a common occurrence in persons who have indulged in a little too much alcohol."

Josephina's cheeks turned pink. "In which case I shall never drink again."

"Hmm, I've heard that one before," said Dominic, but without question there was a hint of amusement in his eyes.

Anna sighed. "I don't know about never drinking again, but I'm certainly never going to eat pizza again. Not before bedtime anyway."

Maci looked concerned. "Anyway, pizza aside, we're going to St Ives today, Anna, and Jo's coming with us because Dominic's doing some of his weird stuff. Would you like to come too?"

"That's very sweet of you but I think I'd like to have a quiet lazy day. Thank you for asking me though."

"Weird stuff," said Dominic, peering over the top of his glasses, "I'll have you know, young lady that I shall be meeting up with a gentleman this afternoon who shares my enthusiasm for life in the hereafter, and not doing weird stuff."

Maci giggled. "Sounds weird to me, but I'm sorry if I've offended you."

To everyone's surprise, Dominic laughed. "Your apology, my dear, is accepted."

Later that morning, Poppy, conscious that it would soon be time to return to university, reluctantly admitted that she really ought to do a little studying to prepare herself for the new academic year.

"Will you be alright on your own for a while?" she asked Anna. "It'll only be for a few hours and so we can go out later. Perhaps to the pub again." She giggled. "We might actually see your stranger from the train this time."

Anna smiled awkwardly at the mention of the strange man but said nothing of her dream to Poppy for fear of ridicule.

"Yes, I'll be fine, really I will. In fact I shall probably take a nice long walk and explore a little more of the town or perhaps even take a stroll along the beach. It might help clear my fuzzy head."

"Oh no, poor you, are you feeling a bit rough?"

"Hmm, just a little but I think lack of sleep is to blame more than drinking. As I said to Jo this morning, pizza before bed is not a good idea. At least, for me it isn't."

Anna left the house by the front door and before she left the premises she walked down through the gardens. By the pond she paused and looked into the sparkling clear water. No fish were visible darting amongst the duckweed and the water lilies but to her delight a beautiful dragonfly was hovering over the lily pads. She watched it, mesmerised, until it flew away.

Before she headed for the driveway, Anna glanced around the garden, hopeful of seeing Rafe who might accompany her on her walk, but he was with Alfie who was up a ladder picking apples with James and so Anna headed for the driveway alone. Before she reached the gate she looked back at the house and its three chimneys standing tall beneath the fast moving clouds. She smiled, relieved to see they looked far less sinister in the cold light of day.

Anna recalled that during one of her walks around Penzance she had seen the tower of a church and so headed downhill in search of it. She eventually found the Parish Church of Saint Mary the Virgin at the bottom of the town and overlooking the sea. She entered the churchyard through an open wrought iron gate, but instantly realised that the graveyard bore no resemblance at all to that in her dream. There was no horse chestnut tree or any evidence of freshly dug earth and in looking further, Anna found that no-one had been buried there since the 1800s. Disappointed, yet also relieved, Anna left through a gate beside the church tower. It was twelve o'clock.

With plenty of time on her hands, Anna slowly ambled towards the town and browsed the shops in the Causewayhead. Feeling peckish, she bought a currant bun and then continued to walk on in the direction of The Old Tile House.

Away from the shops, she passed by drystone walls overgrown with nettles, brambles and ivy. At the top of the hill she looked back towards the distant coastline, which was almost identical to the view from her bedroom window.

On reaching the turning that would eventually take her back to The Old Tile House, Anna momentarily paused, for something in her subconscious urged her not to return to the guest house but to walk on. She followed her instincts and continued along the road, passing more drystone walls which sprouted ferns and red valerian. As she stopped to pick a stem of the red flowers, she saw a group of tall trees towering overhead and swaying beneath the pale blue sky. She put the flower into the button hole of her jacket and then continued on along the path and around a bend. Suddenly she came to a halt. In front of her was Penzance Cemetery.

Anna took smaller steps as she neared the entrance and cautiously peered inside. Towards her, beneath the trees, a fleet of black cars were creeping along the tarmac. She stepped aside as they emerged through the gate and drove by. Her head bowed low until they were out of sight.

Timorously, Anna walked through a deep archway that ran through a building which she imagined to be a house. From there she proceeded towards the canopy of the tall trees that she had observed from the path outside. She glanced around: the cemetery was huge. Following a path she stopped by a silver birch. Not far away gravediggers were already beginning the sad task of covering someone's remains.

Anna kept her distance. She hid in the shadows and looked at the tombstones of very old graves. Some had subsided, others were lifted by the force of large tree roots. She bent to smell a deep, red rose and then glanced over her shoulder. The gravediggers were chatting as they worked.

To pass the time, she sat down on a green, iron bench and ruffled through the contents of her brown, leather handbag on pretence of looking for something. She pulled out her phone and pretended to be engrossed in it while she waited for the gravediggers to leave. It was very peaceful sitting in the September sunshine. Restful too and very quiet.

Finally they went, spades over shoulders, talking quietly. Anna rose from the bench and when they were out of sight she slowly strolled along the gravel path, her heart thumping loudly with every step that she took. As she neared the spot where the men had been working, blood drained from her face, for ahead of her was the laurel bush that she had seen in her dream and beside it lay a heaped mass of brightly, coloured flowers.

After looking over her shoulder to see that no-one was around, she nervously knelt down to read the cards attached to the wreaths adorning the mysterious grave.

Dearest William, she read, *God be with you. Belinda and Kevin.*

Goodbye William Carthew, a fine friend over these many years. John.

Fondest love, dear William. Uncle Henry.

You've been a wonderful, son, William. We shall never forget you. Love and kisses. Mum and Dad.

And so the messages went on. But who was William Carthew besides being a son, a nephew and a friend?

Anna read a few more of the cards and then stood up. Her head was spinning and her mind felt addled. Feeling the sudden desperate need to get away from the sombre surroundings, she fled back down the path and shuffled through a few early fallen leaves. Without stopping she ran beneath the archway and back out into the street, glad to see traffic and people walking along the pavement.

When she reached The Old Tile House, she jumped on finding Alfie on his knees brushing flakes of paint from the iron gates at the foot of the driveway. At first he laughed but then became concerned when he saw the confused and worried look on her pale face and noticed that she was shaking.

He stood up. "Are you alright, Anna? I hope I haven't startled you."

"No, no, you haven't. Well, that is I didn't expect to see you there and so you made me jump because I was miles away, but really I'm fine." She looked at the wire brush in his hand. "Are…are you going to paint the gates?" She stammered, eager to direct the subject away from her apprehension.

"Yes, we've been saying all summer that they need doing. I'm not doing them today though; I'll do it next week when there are fewer guests. We can't have you getting paint on your fine clothes." He tried to be jovial.

"No, no, of course not."

"Anyway, I've finished as much as I can do today."

"Yes, that's good."

Alfie walked with Anna along the drive and up towards the house. "So, where have you been? Out walking?"

"What? Oh, yes, yes, I've just been wandering around the town and so forth." Anna was hesitant for a few seconds and then asked on impulse, "Does the name William Carthew mean anything to you, Alfie?"

He shook his head. "Can't say that it does. Should it?"

"No, no, I suppose not. I just heard the name mentioned whilst out and it seemed to ring a bell," she lied.

Alfie nodded thoughtfully. "Hmm, probably some sort of celeb. I must admit there are loads of them that I've never heard of. And even some that are household names are a mystery to me because I've not the foggiest idea who they are or why they're famous. I must be getting old."

Anna smiled, weakly. "Yes, same here."

At the top of the drive Alfie walked over to the tool shed and put the wire brush inside. He then walked with Anna round to the front of the house where Poppy was sitting on the steps looking at her mobile phone.

Poppy looked up when she heard their feet crunching across the gravel. "Oh, there you are. I've been looking everywhere for you, Anna."

"Oh, any particular reason?"

Poppy shook her head. "No, I just wondered if you were back from your walk but obviously you weren't."

"I see, yes, well I only just got back and then found Alfie brushing the gates."

"And now I must go and water the tomatoes," said Alfie, "bye, girls."

"You two make a really sweet couple," teased Poppy, as Alfie crossed the lawn towards the greenhouse.

"What?"

"Don't pretend you're surprised by my comment, Anna Greenwood," said Poppy, grinning broadly. "I mean, let's be honest, you both like flowers and stuff like that and you just look…well…um… well suited. It's a pity that you're not here for a little longer."

Anna felt her face flush. "I think your imagination is running a little riot, Poppy, because I'm sure Alfie only sees me as another one of the guests, hence his courtesy."

"Hmm, possibly, but how do you see him, I wonder."

Anna opened her mouth to reply but to her surprise it was a question she was unable to answer.

In the evening Anna, not feeling very sociable, feigned a headache and stayed in her room and watched television. For not only was she feeling desperately tired and looking forward to an early night, she was also repelled by the prospect of drinking wine as would be the case if she were to venture into the guests' lounge.

By nine o' clock she was bored with the television and so switched it off. Not quite ready for bed, she sat down on the south facing window seat, with the window wide open so that she could breathe in some fresh air. Outside the garden was in darkness and there were no stars or moon in the cloudy sky. All was quiet except for the whispering of the weeping willow's leaves as they rustled in a gentle breeze.

Anna thought back to Poppy's words regarding herself and Alfie. To her surprise she found the prospect of knowing him better filled her with a pleasant warmth. She half-smiled, saddened by the knowledge that the likelihood of a romance blossoming was out of the question for she was due to return home on Sunday and so had only four days of her holiday left.

Chapter Thirteen

Anna woke up on Wednesday morning and sighed; it was her twenty third birthday. Wondering if she had any messages from her friends and work colleagues, she sat up in bed and looked at her phone to check Facebook. To her delight, several people had already sent their good wishes and it wasn't even eight o'clock.

Anna stretched her arms and then picked up Andy. "I've a feeling that today is going to be really, really special, Andy Bear," she said, kissing the top of his furry head, "and if it is you'll be the first to hear all about it."

She sat him down on top of her pillows and then stepped out of bed, happy with the knowledge that she had not dreamed and had slept well. Two very good reasons she considered as excuse enough to celebrate.

With a spring in her step she went into the bathroom, determined to put behind her all the weird happenings of the past few days and to enjoy every moment of her special day.

As she came out of the bathroom, she again recalled Poppy's comment about her and Alfie making a nice couple. Anna glanced at the roses. Was there really any truth in Poppy's opinion and if so was it possible that Alfie had sneaked into her room with the flowers in the dead of night? Anna thought it unlikely but at the same time with Alfie doing maintenance work to the house then it would not be unreasonable to suspect he may have found the secret door that linked the two wardrobes.

Anna crossed the room and touched the velvety flowers half hoping that her surmise might bear some truth.

When she went down for breakfast the other guests were already seated and in turn all wished her many happy returns of the day. Anna thanked them for their good wishes even though she was surprised that they even knew. Certainly she had told Poppy earlier in the week that she was almost twenty three but she hadn't expected her to have told anyone else. Not that Anna minded. Deep down she was thrilled.

As Anna sat at her usual table, Josephina announced that if she were willing they would like to take her out for a birthday lunch. Anna felt the backs of her eyes prickle and said that she would be delighted.

Seven went out for lunch: Josephina, Dominic, Meldrick, Maci, Alfie, who had the day off, Poppy and Anna who wore her new dress. Brenda and Brian would have joined the group but they had already booked a day trip to the Isles of Scilly and they couldn't change it because it was their last day. However, they insisted that they must all have a small gathering in the evening which would be a combination of Anna's birthday celebrations and a last evening drink for themselves.

As the birthday group left The Old Tile House by way of the front door, Anna was amused to see Rafe and Henry lying side by side gazing into the pond. She pointed them out to Alfie.

"Yeah, they often do that. I think they're mesmerised by the fish."

"I hope they don't try to catch them," said Josephina.

Alfie shook his head. "No, I think they're both very much aware of their limitations and I know for a fact that Henry was unfortunate enough to discover he wasn't a fan of water earlier this year when he happened to wander in the path of the lawn sprinkler."

"Oh, poor Henry," said Anna, as the cat raised his head having heard mention of his name. "Am I right in thinking that moggies are not over fond of getting wet?"

"Big cats living in very hot climates are glad of water to cool them down," said Maci, "but domestic cats aren't so keen, especially if the weather is chilly."

Alfie chuckled. "Hmm, Henry got wet on a chilly day. It was back in the spring when the sprinkler was watering freshly laid turf."

Maci tutted. "Oh dear, poor pussykins."

"Maci's soppy about cats," said Meldrick, as they all made their way towards the driveway, "aren't you, my love?"

"Absolutely. In fact were it possible I'd like to come back as a cat in another life."

"Well, if you do then I shall come back as a dog and chase you," said Meldrick, affectionately slapping her bottom.

"What would you like to come back as, Anna?" Alfie asked.

"What? Oh, I don't really know, but I wouldn't want to be an animal so I suppose it would have to be a human and a female one at that."

"Hear, hear," said Josephina, "the life span of animals is far too short and I should hate to get dirty and not be able to shower."

"Women and their female logic," said Meldrick, with a hearty laugh, "that's what I love about them."

As they neared the bottom of the driveway where their taxi was waiting, it suddenly occurred to Anna that Dominic had not spoken once as they'd walked along the gravel drive but had indeed looked sorrowful just as Josephina had maintained. She frowned, curious to know what it was about that particular part of The Old Tile House grounds that saddened him so.

The birthday group had opted to have lunch at the Crown and Anchor in Pentrillick, because Poppy had said that Anna liked both the village and its pub, and it was also a firm favourite of Alfie's. Anna thought it was a very thoughtful choice and was happy to return there for a second visit. They had chosen to go by taxi so that everyone could have a drink.

Because there was a cool breeze blowing they decided to sit inside the pub rather than out on the beer terrace, but chose a table near to open French doors so that they could both view and hear the sound of the sea and the cry of the gulls.

Before their meals arrived, they each raised their glasses of wine and toasted the birthday girl who sat directly opposite Dominic. Anna, overwhelmed by their good wishes, nervously laughed and heartily thanked them all, but as Dominic lowered his glass and smiled at Anna, her laughter faded and she found her eyes transfixed on his face. For in his warm smile she detected an unexpected pang of recognition: a flash of familiarity as though she had known him sometime in the past. But then the feeling vanished just as quickly as it had arrived and once again she saw him as a casual acquaintance.

After the meal, they each had a coffee, during which Meldrick pointed to a piano standing at the far end of the bar. "I wonder if they ever have sing-songs in here like pubs did in days gone by."

"Doubt it," said Josephina, "shame really I should imagine they were quite good fun."

"I've been in here loads of times," said Alfie, "and I've never even seen the piano opened up."

"That's sad," said Maci, "I like the sound of a piano. Mum had loads of Richard Clayderman LPs when we were kids and she was always playing them."

Dominic looked at Anna. "Why don't you play us a tune, Anna? Something relaxing, Chopin maybe. I'm sure the landlord wouldn't mind as there are very few people in here now."

Anna froze. "What makes you think that I can play?"

"Probably because you have long fingers," said Josephina, with a nod of her head, "Dominic always says that's the case with pianists."

Anna looked at her fingers. "I'm sure they're no longer than anyone else's."

Poppy held up her hand and rested it flat against Anna's. "No, that can't be right," she said with a giggle, "Our fingers are exactly the same length and I'm musically tone deaf."

"That's as maybe," said Dominic, "but Anna can play." He started to hum *Nocturne*.

"Stop it," said Anna, as her heart thumped loudly, "you're freaking me out. How did you know that I could play the piano? Not that I can very well. I mean, I've never had lessons but I can pick out tunes and play by ear."

"Landlord, may my friend give us a quick tune on your piano?" Dominic asked the man standing behind the bar.

"Please do, it's seldom used these days which is a shame, but it should be in tune because funnily enough, we had it done last week."

"Yay, go on, Anna, give us a tune," said Maci. "Something jolly."

Anna slowly stood in order to make her way to the far end of the bar. "Is it, is it unlocked?" she nervously asked the landlord, who was stacking clean glasses on a shelf.

"Yes, love. We never lock it as we don't have a key. The piano was here when we took the pub over so the key's probably been lost for a while."

"I see, thank you."

Recalling the dream that she had dreamt while in the summerhouse, Anna slowly continued towards the piano. A feeling of unease crept over her as she realised the piano was as dark as ebony and that it stood in a dimly lit corner beside an exposed stone wall. Apprehensively, she pulled out the stool, sat down and slowly lifted the lid. But even before she began to contemplate playing, she saw that three of the keys were chipped. Three in a row. The same ones as in her dream.

Anna changed into a pair of comfortable shoes and her favourite jeans after they arrived back at The Old Tile House after which she went out for a walk with Poppy. She said nothing of the chipped piano keys, nor did she mention her dream but instead focused her attention on asking Poppy about her friends at university and the subject she was studying even though science was of no interest to her.

On their return Anna went up to her room and laid down on her bed. After looking at Facebook on her phone, where she saw several more friends and colleagues had sent birthday greetings, she switched on the television and watched it for a while. After the local news, she changed back into her new dress which she had worn earlier for lunch and then touched up her make-up.

Before going down to the lounge she knelt on the window seat. The sun was setting over the sea in a glorious array of amber, gold and dusky pink. She watched, mesmerised as the radiant orb disappeared until only a faint glimmer of pastel shades coloured the darkening sky. Thrilled to have witnessed the sunset, Anna then went down to the lounge where other guests were already gathered for her birthday and a farewell drink with Brenda and Brian.

Margot and Hugo, also in the lounge and drinking white wine, wished Anna a happy birthday. Anna graciously thanked them. They seemed really nice and she regretted that they too were going home the following day.

Alfie smiled as Anna looked his way and after he handed her a drink they sat down together on the hearth rug.

Brenda and Brian, having had a lovely day on the Isles of Scilly, sat on the small settee, sipping red wine and enjoying the warmth of the fire lit earlier in the day by Michelle, for the nights were beginning to feel a little chilly.

"Gosh, quite a roomful," said Poppy, on entering the lounge and placing three bottles of wine on the sideboard sent with her parents' compliments.

"Margot was just telling us how she knew this house when she was a girl," said Brenda, excitedly, "Isn't that fascinating?"

"Really," said Poppy, sitting down on the arm of the large settee where Margot and Hugo were seated, "when was that?"

"Oh gosh, years and years ago long before you were born, dear. It was my aunt and uncle's house and they lived here along with my two cousins. Of course they were only children then like myself, the cousins, that is, not my aunt and uncle." She sighed deeply. "Poor Cousin William, it was to his funeral that we went yesterday."

"Oh, I am sorry," said Poppy, surprised, "I didn't even realise that you'd been to a funeral."

Margot patted Poppy's arm in a reassuring manner. "Nor should you have, dear. It would have been most unfair of us to bring sadness to this house when your guests are all here to enjoy themselves. But what's done now is done and yesterday's sorrow will slowly fade."

"I take it your cousin was no age then," said Brian, feeling a little subdued himself because it was their last evening, "assuming he was a similar age to yourself, that is."

"Quite right. Indeed we were of a similar age," said Margot, "I'm forty seven and William was forty six."

"Dear, dear," said Meldrick, "that's no age at all. So did the unfortunate chap suffer from poor health?"

Margot shook her head. "As far as I know he enjoyed relatively good health but he died suddenly about ten days ago after a brief illness. I must admit I'd not seen him for many years: not since we were children in fact. He'd lived in Penzance all his life and I'm told that it was his dying wish that he be buried here."

"So, did he still have family down here?" Maci asked.

"Oh yes," said Margot, "his parents still live in the town now. After they left here which must be coming up for twenty years ago, they moved into a much smaller house and at the same time, William also bought his own place somewhere in the town. I believe he was an accountant and so was earning quite well."

As Margot spoke, Hugo looked quizzically at Dominic. "Please don't think me rude, but didn't I see you at the funeral yesterday? Because if it wasn't you then you have a double."

Dominic awkwardly half-smiled. "Well, yes, yes, actually it was me," he said, "I was there." He bit his bottom lip and looked uncomfortable as he glanced at Josephina whose eyebrows were raised as far as was physically possible.

"You went to a funeral. But you told me you were meeting someone who shared your thoughts of life in the hereafter or something like that," said Josephina, feeling her cheeks begin to flush, "Why on earth didn't you tell me that's where you were really going?"

Dominic looked downcast. "Because you seemed to be enjoying our holiday, my love, and I thought you might think attending a funeral would be a little dull and depressing to say the least."

Josephina tutted. "That's very sweet of you but I would have understood and I'm surprised that you didn't realise that."

"Yes, in retrospect I'm sure that you wouldn't have minded." He gripped her hand firmly. "I'm sorry for my dishonesty. Really, I am."

Josephina kissed his cheek. "Silly you. You're forgiven but who was this William and when did he die? I obviously know that he was Margot's cousin, but how did you know him and did you know that he'd died when you booked our stay here?"

"No, when I suggested this break he was still alive, but he died soon after." Dominic gulped, clearly upset, "But as soon as I realised that he'd gone, I knew that I had to be at his funeral."

"So when did you find out?" Josephina asked, "I'm really confused. And how come you'd never mentioned that you knew someone who had once lived in this house?"

Dominic took a deep breath. "I realised he had gone the minute we arrived here. It was uncanny. I felt his presence the moment I stepped through the door."

Brenda gasped. "Really? So this house is haunted." She slapped her knee. "I suspected as much."

"Haunted?" Dominic laughed nervously. "No, Brenda, it isn't haunted. William has gone now," he whispered.

Anna felt uncomfortable as Dominic turned and looked in her direction.

"Do you by any chance have a photograph of your cousin?" he suddenly asked Margot.

"Why, yes," said Margot, "I have yesterday's Order of Service sheet and it has a lovely picture of William on the front which I believe was taken earlier this year."

"Yes, I recall admiring it," Dominic agreed, confidence having returned to his voice, "but stupidly I left my service sheet in the church."

Margot reached for her handbag and rummaged through its contents. "Ah, here it is," she said, lifting out the sheet and handing it to Dominic.

"William Francis Carthew," he read, "and what a fine looking man he was. Do you not agree?" He handed the sheet to Josephina who concurred with his statement and then passed it on around the room.

Anna could hear her heart thumping as the sheet slowly made its way towards her.

"So when and for how long did you know William?" Margot asked, returning her handbag to the floor beside her feet.

"We met as new boys at secondary school and became best friends on that very first day and have been friends ever since. I like to think we were kindred spirits. Of course, I also knew this house when William was a boy and during our schooldays I became a frequent visitor."

As Dominic spoke Anna suddenly became aware that he was wearing the same flamboyant waistcoat as on the first day that she had seen him. It had red buttons with diamanté centres and one was now missing. Her head began to spin. Was it Dominic that she had sensed in her room in the middle of the night? If so why had he been in there? And what about the mysterious appearance of yellow roses the following night. Was Dominic in any way involved with their materialisation?

In a daze Anna turned her head towards Margot who was speaking. "And William never married," she said, "because sadly he lost all interest in women after poor Emily died. Dear, dear, such unfortunate circumstances although I regret that I'm unable to remember all the details. I just recall that it was a pretty dreadful affair. Poor, poor, Emily."

"I remember it as if it were yesterday," said Dominic, dreamily, "even though it was twenty three years ago. Poor Emily Penlow, she was only twenty one years old when she died. She was as pretty as a picture and William adored her and she adored him. She had a heart of gold and tried so hard to help William get over the loss of a previous girlfriend. After she died William became very introverted and who could blame him? Such a dreadful thing to have happened and he was riddled with guilt. He was still here living with his parents when I left Cornwall twenty one years ago and even though we'd always kept in touch, I never saw him again in the flesh and I deeply regret that."

"Where did Emily live?" Anna asked, as the chipped piano keys flashed into her mind.

"She lived here in Pentrillick," said Dominic, "and often did a few shifts at the Crown and Anchor where funnily enough we were earlier today."

"Really," said Poppy, eyes like saucers, "how weird that we should have gone there today of all days."

Dominic nodded. "Yes, isn't it?"

"How…how did Emily die?" Anna asked, as the Order of Service sheet fell into her clammy hands.

"She died in a tragic accident," said Dominic, carefully watching Anna's face as she recognised William Carthew on the Order of Service sheet as being the mysterious man on the train. "It was an accident that happened here out on the driveway."

Poppy gasped. "No, surely not."

"So, so what happened?" asked Brenda, placing her wine glass on an occasional table lest she spill it.

"Emily was going to go out for a ride with William on the back of his brand new motorcycle," said Dominic, "He was very proud of that bike and said that she must be the first person he took out for a spin. Sadly she was not only the first but also the last. You see, the scarf she was wearing around her neck got caught in the back wheel of the vehicle and when William drove it away, she was strangled. I was there and I witnessed it. It was horrible. We tried to resuscitate her as did the paramedics who arrived very quickly, but our efforts were all in vain and she died out there on the gravel."

No-one spoke as Dominic fiddled with the strap of his watch and gazed absently into space. "After that poor William never rode the motorcycle again. In fact, he gave it away because he couldn't even bear to look at it."

Brenda's voice was little more than a whisper, "How horrible."

Josephina hugged Dominic tightly. "Why on earth didn't you tell me? Poor Emily. "You obviously knew her well also. Why have you tormented yourself like this in silence?"

He nodded. "Because...because, I don't know, I just did." Slowly his eyes filled with tears. "I suppose that up until now I was unable to speak about it. Relive it. And with William gone too...." His voice faded.

During the general uttering of hushed words of condolence and compassion that followed, Anna's face turned from an embarrassed pink to a deathly white, and the sound of her quickened heart rate thumped loudly through her spinning head. As she sat, her mind racing with muddled thoughts, she suddenly remembered the other grave in her dream. The one with the yellow roses beneath the horse chestnut tree.

"Excuse me," she said in a voice that was not her own as she unsteadily rose to her feet and dropped the Order of Service sheet onto Alfie's lap. Without saying where she was going or why, she left the room, and fled from the house into the cool night air.

Rafe, out in the garden saw her leaving and followed as she ran towards the driveway. Half way down she paused and listened as the leaves on the trees and shrubs eerily whispered all around her. She span around and looked up to the waving branches and then ran in panic down the rest of the driveway and out onto the pavement. Rafe followed at her heels as she ran through the streets. Neither girl nor dog stopped until they reached the cemetery.

As Anna staggered breathlessly, beneath the cemetery's deep archway, a misty drizzle began to fall from the darkening sky and overhead the dying leaves of the trees rustled in a freshening wind. Shivering, for her dress had no sleeves, Anna walked quickly until she reached the gravel path leading to William Carthew's grave and from there she crept slowly towards the mound of fresh flowers.

Standing beside the now familiar laurel bush, she glanced intensely around looking for the horse chestnut tree that she had seen in her dream. In the semi-darkness, she spotted it over in a quiet corner. It was huge.

Frozen to the spot, Anna looked up at its long branches, each one heavy with conkers, not yet ripe. Then with thumping heart, she slowly tip-toed towards it, careful to avoid treading on the neglected graves. Under the tree, just as in her dream, yellow roses graced an urn beneath a polished granite headstone.

Lowering her head, she touched the roses and then bent to read the inscription:

In loving memory of
Emily Samantha Penlow.
So cruelly taken from us.
Born June 7th 1969
Died September 11th 1990.
R.I.P.

Anna leapt back in horror as she realised why she had always felt compelled to visit Penzance. Emily's death had occurred on the day that she was born. As she stared at the headstone, her neck began to tingle and burn. Her throat felt restricted and her lifelong fear of choking intensified. Shocked by the revelation of a past life, she attempted to scream, but no sound emerged from her white lips. Petrified, she began to run; stumbling over graves, slipping on moss, damp through living in constant shade. In the semi-darkness she tore the skirt of her dress on a bramble and stained the fabric with juice from the wild berries. And then she saw him standing beside the laurel bush. Beside his own grave. William Carthew, just as he had looked on the train. He smiled as she looked in his direction and held out his hands. Anna gasped, unsure, confused. Rafe barked. What should she do? But then she surrendered, mesmerised by his pleading eyes and without another thought she hurriedly stepped towards him. In haste, her foot caught on a gnarled root of a tree. She flung out her arms but there was nothing to grab. She heard William shout and then rush towards her, but he was too late. She fell forwards and hit her head heavily against the corner of a broken, jagged tombstone.

Barking loudly, Rafe ran around in circles and then stopped and crouched down beside Anna's motionless body. He whimpered and then lovingly licked her white face and the blood that slowly trickled from her lacerated forehead.

Overhead, the dark clouds dispersed, the wind abated and the moon emerged and shone down, throwing ghostly shadows across the endless rows of crooked tombstones.

Chapter Fourteen

Through a misty haze, Anna saw William Carthew bend over her and lift her up into his arms. Effortlessly, he carried her through the clouds towards a bright light, looked on by angels singing and cherubs playing shiny brass trumpets. Colourful flowers cascaded from majestic urns which reposed upon marble pedestals and overhead tall trees rustled with golden leaves which sparkled in the brilliance of the nearing light. In a gentle breeze, silver bells jingled and sprinkled glitter over the wings of the angels whose voices rang out through the misty atmosphere. And as he laid her down on a golden couch scattered with pointed white feathers, Anna heard herself ask, "Am I dead?"

A familiar chuckle caused her to force open her heavy eyelids.

"No, my sweetheart, you're very much alive."

Anna slowly turned her aching head towards Alfie's voice and saw him sitting beside her. "What happened?" she asked, reaching out for his hand.

He took both her hands in his and gently kissed them. "When you left so abruptly we were all alarmed and so I asked Dominic where you were going. Poor man he was as white as a sheet and said that you were going to the cemetery. We had no idea why and so we followed you there."

"What, all of you?"

"Yes, all of us, even Margot and Hugo."

Anna leaned back onto three pillows and looked at the screens that enclosed the bed upon which she was lying. "Judging by my surroundings I assume that I'm in a hospital."

"Yes, you are, but don't worry, you're going to be fine. The gash on your head is superficial and will heal and may not even leave a scar."

She squeezed his hands. "How long have I been here?"

"About four hours. The others went back to The Old Tile House as soon as they knew you were okay. I said I'd stay with you until you woke up."

"Oh, Alfie, I thought I was dead again."

"Again," said Alfie, puzzled, "what do you mean by again?"

"I died once before, twenty three years ago. You see, I am the reincarnation of Emily Penlow. I must be because I was born on the day that she died. William Carthew wanted me to follow him into the hereafter but I've come back. He was very sweet and I hope he's not cross." She began to cry.

Alfie smiled and lovingly brushed away her tears. "In reality, you never went anywhere, my sweetheart. You were knocked unconscious for a short while and have been sleeping for an hour or two now, but it was only in your dreams that you left planet Earth."

"But..."

"...Dominic will explain everything to you tomorrow after you've been discharged. Meanwhile, you must get more rest and so must I." He leaned over and kissed her cheek. "I'll tell the nurses that you're awake now and then be back in the morning to see when you can come home."

"Home?"

"Well, you know, The Old Tile House."

Anna smiled. "I shall look forward to seeing you."

It was early evening of the following day before Anna was finally discharged from hospital and as Alfie drove her towards The Old Tile House she noticed the pavements were wet and the darkening sky was grey. As they drove along the driveway, she shuddered recalling the demise of Emily Penlow and attempted to banish from her mind the picture of Emily's death that her imagination repeatedly conjured up.

Inside the house, Michelle was waiting and ushered them both into the guests' lounge where a fire had been lit since lunchtime to safeguard the patient's wellbeing.

News of Anna's return quickly spread amongst the guests and soon all were by her side excitedly chattering and saying how glad they were to see her up and about.

As Anna sat down on the settee nearest the fire she was surprised to see Brenda who handed her a mug of tea after Poppy had wrapped a woollen shawl around her shoulders. "Brenda, how come you and Brian are still here? I thought you were going home today."

"That was the plan," said Brenda, rubbing her hands excitedly, "but there's no way we were leaving here until we knew that all was well with you. Brian phoned the pub last night and asked our wonderful staff to hold the fort for another day. He told them he'd explain why when we got back."

"Oh, that's really sweet of you, but as you can see, I'm fine."

"I'm sure you are," said Brenda, sitting on the arm of the small settee, "but we wanted to see…no, no, I mustn't speak out of turn."

Anna glanced around the room at the eager faces. "What's going on? I sense an air of anticipation amongst you all."

"Very perceptive of you, my dear," said Dominic, as he moved away from the table near the window and knelt down by her feet.

Anna frowned as she looked into his blue eyes and recalled the feeling of having known him sometime in her past. "You must all think me very silly for believing I was the reincarnation of Emily Penlow." She half smiled, "in retrospect I also think I was daft. But it all made sense when I was there in the cemetery last night. You know, my fear of choking, the feelings of déjà vu, seeing William Carthew, you knowing I played the piano and the feeling I had of having known you long ago. The thing is, if I'm not Emily nor ever have been, why did all those strange things happen to me?"

The room was silent except for the crackling of the fire and the glugging sound of wine as Brian poured Dominic a second glass and a third for himself.

Dominic nodded his thanks to Brian and took a sip before he spoke. "As I said last night, William and I first met when we went to secondary school. We hit it off instantly because we both had limited psychic powers which drew us together and at the same time it segregated us from the rest of our contemporaries." Dominic laughed, recalling his school days. "Thankfully the isolation didn't last long and the rest of our class mates soon became fascinated with some of the things we were able to tell them. Although, I must admit at times we were a little economical with the truth and they were all very disappointed that neither of us was able to foresee questions which might arise in future exam papers thus enabling them to be prepared with the correct answers." He took another sip of wine and then stood the glass on the hearth. "But that doesn't answer your questions, does it?"

Anna shook her head.

"After we left school, William studied to be an accountant and I trained to be a surveyor. We were both successful and were both still friends although we spent far less time together than we had done during our school days. Nevertheless, whenever we could we would meet up and go out for a drink together and Emily often went with us. One of our favourite pubs was the Crown and Anchor at Pentrillick. The pub was run by David and Grace Penlow and they had a son called Jonathan who had been in the same tutor group as William and I when we were at school. Back then, Emily was at college and so to earn some money in her spare time, the Penlows offered her a few evening's work on the bar. And then before we knew it, Emily and Jonathan had fallen madly in love and they married the following summer. Which would have been the summer of 1988."

"Stop, stop a minute," said Anna, raising her hand, "because I'm getting muddled already. You just said that Emily married Jonathan, which would certainly make her a Penlow, but I thought that she was William Carthew's girlfriend and Penlow was her maiden name. I'm really confused."

Dominic shook his head. "No, no, Emily Penlow was formerly Emily Carthew and she was William's little sister."

Anna slumped back into the cushions of the settee. "Oh, but that's dreadful. So, poor William lost his sister and not his girlfriend. What a horrible situation for him to have been in."

"Yes," said Dominic, "it was. But of course that's not the end of the story, nor even the middle. Would you like me to continue?"

"Yes, of course. Sorry I interrupted."

"No, you were right to do so because we all want you to understand what I'm telling you."

Anna laughed nervously. "That sounds a little ominous."

Dominic patted her hand in a reassuring manner. "I can promise you that it is not. Anyway, to continue. After their marriage, Emily and Jonathan, bought a small cottage in Pentrillick and because Jonathan, when he had lived at home in the pub had helped out in his spare time, Grace and David decided they would need extra help with him gone, especially during the holiday season and so they advertised. At the beginning of the Easter holidays in 1989, they took on a new girl not of the village who they accommodated in Jonathan's old room. And then lo and behold, she too became one of our friends and especially so with William." Dominic chuckled, "he was besotted with her the moment he first saw her and everyone instantly thought that his days of being a bachelor were numbered, but sadly, she didn't stay. After New Year's Eve she left for London and we never saw her again.

After she went William was heartbroken but eventually time healed his wounds. Emily was a great comfort to him and gradually she enticed him to get out and about again. And then, as you already know, Emily died and William's world fell apart." Dominic took another sip of wine and then continued. "David and Grace left the Crown and Anchor many years ago and moved here to Penzance. Needless to say, living up-country, I'd not seen them for years but when I arrived here and heard of William's death, I had good reason to look them up and that's where I went on Monday when you girls were out shopping and partaking of a little too much alcohol. I asked them about the girl they'd employed in 1989 because all I could remember was that we called her Andy."

"Andy," said Brenda, "but that's not a girl's name."

"Bear with me," said Dominic, "and all will be revealed." He took a deep breath. "Grace and David remembered Andy well, after all she did work for them for almost a year. They told me that prior to coming to Cornwall she'd lived in Devon and Somerset and had been adopted when she was a just few weeks old. Her name was Amanda Greenwood."

Anna's hands felt clammy and her heart began to race. "Mum," she whispered, "my mother was William Carthew's girlfriend."

Dominic nodded. "Yes."

"And so…so, is, was, William my father?"

"Yes. William always said that he knew somewhere out there he had a daughter but he didn't know where and it grieved him."

"But how did he know?"

Dominic smiled. "He just did. Just as you knew this house and the pub at Pentrillick. Just as I knew you could play the piano and you thought you knew me. Just as he did, you love yellow roses."

"You're clairvoyant, dear," said Brenda, "don't you think that's exciting?"

"What...oh, I...I don't know what to think." She turned to Dominic. "Did you put the roses in my room?"

Dominic laughed. "Yes, I did and I'm sorry if it frightened you. That was the night we'd been to the ghost hunt. Josephina fell asleep as soon as we got back but I was wide awake and so crept out and cut the flowers. I took them to your room through the wardrobe, having already checked out that you were in the right room the night before. I knew my actions would meet with William's approval, especially as the roses in question were planted by him."

Josephina tutted.

"You naughty boy," said Brenda, thoroughly enjoying the narrative.

Anna looked thoughtful. "And so what happened at the cemetery?" she asked. "Did William...my father, want me to go to with him?"

Dominic shook his head. "No, sweetheart, he just wanted to hug you before he went away himself."

"And Emily...if she was William's sister, then, then...she was...." Anna was unable to finish the sentence.

"Yes," said Dominic, "she was your aunt."

"Would you like a glass of wine, Anna?" Brenda asked, "You're looking awfully pale."

Anna nodded. "Yes, please, Brenda. I think I need one."

Anna said nothing as she quietly sipped her wine and everyone else spoke in hushed tones.

Eventually Anna spoke, "It all makes sense now. When I was young I wanted to come to Cornwall for a holiday and Penzance in particular but Mum said no and that Devon was just as nice. I suppose she wouldn't come back here because of the memories and she knew that my father was here. Also, she must have taken me to see *The Pirates of Penzance* because deep down she loved the place too. But why didn't she tell William about me? That's what I don't understand."

"Perhaps she didn't know about you herself until after she'd left Pentrillick," said Brenda, "the dates would add up."

"Or she didn't want to make William feel obliged to take care of you and her," said Poppy, "from what you've told me of her she seemed very headstrong and independent."

Anna nodded. "Yes, that makes sense. She probably thought William wouldn't want to be tied down with her and a baby and so never made contact. Poor Mum, but sadly she lacked self-esteem. I think that was because she was adopted and so knew nothing of her background. I suppose in a way she thought herself unworthy of William."

"She was certainly modest," said Dominic, "but she was never unworthy. Silly Andy. If only we could turn back the clock."

"Yes," said Anna, "if only." She smiled, dreamily. "You know, I always imagined my father to be a chef and not an accountant but that was simply because my mother worked as a waitress and so would have mixed with people who were wizards with food. Silly, I know, but I thought because I love cooking I might have inherited my skills from him. I certainly didn't get them from Mum because she hated being in the kitchen."

"That's interesting," said Dominic, "but William was certainly no cook either. I don't think he could even boil an egg. Not when I lived in Cornwall anyway although I daresay he made an effort when he had his own place. It was Emily who had the culinary skills and she was doing a catering course at college and hoped one day to have her own restaurant."

"Oh, that's so sad," said Brenda, "poor girl."

"Dominic," said Maci, after a brief moment during which no-one had spoken as they had pondered over Brenda's words, "how did you know who Anna was?"

Dominic's eyes glazed over as her thoughts drifted back. "Because she looks so much like her mother. That evening in here when first we were introduced was like stepping back into the past and the name Greenwood instantly rang a bell. It was really strange hearing Anna speak, her voice was similar to Andy's and so were her mannerisms, yet at the same time she reminded me so much of William and Emily. She has his eyes and his smile and Emily's lovely dark hair. I never had any doubt."

Anna suddenly laughed. "Why did you call Mum Andy?"

Dominic wiped a tear from his eye. "Because the first time we saw her she was working on the bar at the Crown and Anchor. It was Easter Sunday and the place was very busy. William was determined to get to know her and so introduced himself. She was very sweet and told him, when asked, that her name was Mandy but he couldn't hear properly because of the racket and thought she said Andy and the name just stuck."

Anna smiled. "When I was seven, Mum bought me a teddy bear which I still have and treasure. She told me that his name was Andy. Now I know why."

After breakfast, the following morning, Brenda and Brian loaded up their car ready for the drive home.

"I shall miss you all," said Brenda, kissing each in turn, "this really has been a most unusual holiday and I've enjoyed every minute of it."

"We shall miss you too," said Poppy, "we shall all miss you."

"Especially me," said Anna, "I can never thank you enough for all you've done for me this past fortnight."

"It's been a pleasure, dear," said Brenda.

"But never fear," said Brian, slamming shut the door of the boot, "we'll be back next summer and that's a promise. I feel this place is home from home now."

"In which case I shall continue to play cards," said Poppy, "and then next time I might even beat you both. But you must return well before the end of September otherwise I'll be back at uni."

"It's a date," said Brenda, tossing her handbag onto the floor in front of the passenger seat and climbing in after it. "Goodbye all and thank you so much for your hospitality."

"Right, what shall we do today?" asked Alfie, who along with Poppy had been given the day off.

"I think a nice walk is in order as the morning is fine," said Poppy, dramatically looking up to the sky, "but I don't think we should go far because the forecast is for rain later although it's lovely at the moment."

"Excellent idea," Alfie agreed. "What do you think, Anna?"

"Sounds fine," she said. "My head's still up in the clouds so I don't mind what we do."

Rather than go towards the town they walked around a residential area where it was quieter and so they could talk. As they turned into Hillcrest Avenue, Anna's face lit up. "We came this way the other day, didn't we, Poppy? And there's a house along here called Greenwood. Well, actually it's not a house it's a bungalow. You'll love the garden, Alfie, because it's really pretty. I'll show you when we get there."

To Anna's surprise as they reached the garden gate of Greenwood and she raised her hand to point it out to Alfie, the front door opened and Dominic stepped out onto the doorstep. "Hello, you lot," he said as though his presence in the bungalow was nothing unusual, "fancy a coffee?"

"Yes, please," said Poppy and Alfie eagerly in unison as they each took one of Anna's arms and dragged her up the garden path.

"Milk and sugar?" Dominic asked, as he ushered them into a sitting room.

They all nodded.

"Three coffees all with milk and sugar, please and I think I'll have another one too," Dominic called out into the hallway.

"Err...is Jo here?" Anna asked, completely confused. "I mean, what's going on?"

Alfie chuckled and Poppy giggled. Dominic just smiled. "Lovely day," he said, waving his hand towards the window where sunlight streamed in through the large glass panes. "Perhaps we'll have an Indian summer."

"Oh yes, that would be nice," said Poppy, "although I'll not be here to appreciate it as I go back to uni next week."

"And I shall be gone home too," said Dominic.

Anna nodded. "Same here."

"But I shall still be here," said Alfie, cheerfully, "and I agree about an Indian summer. It makes the winter seem so much shorter if we have a nice autumn."

"And then it will be Christmas before we know it," said Poppy, "and I'll be home again."

Alfie nodded. "I do hope there will be berries on the holly this year as last year there were very few."

"That's right. Such a shame because Christmas isn't Christmas without holly."

Anna looked first at Poppy and then at Alfie who had very deliberately placed themselves on either side of her on a large sofa. She was utterly baffled by their strange behaviour and was about to ask if they were feeling alright when a grey haired lady carrying a tea tray entered the room followed by a grey haired man. The lady put the tray down on a table and then turned to greet the visitors.

"So nice of you to call," she said, handing out mugs of coffee from the tea tray.

Anna was even more confused when as she was handed a mug saw that there were tears in the elderly lady's eyes.

"Are you alright?" Anna asked, even though she was oblivious of the reason for the seemingly impromptu meeting.

"Yes, dear, I'm fine," said the lady, "but before I sit I think that we should introduce ourselves." She took hold of the elderly man's hand. "Anna, my dear, we are your grandparents."

Chapter Fifteen

When Anna woke up on Saturday morning the first thing she saw was a photograph of William Carthew standing beside the glass base of her bedside lamp. She picked up the picture and kissed it and then laid her head back on the pillow with the wooden frame firmly clutched in her arms. The picture had been given to her by her grandparents.

"My grandparents," said Anna, relishing the fact she was able to utter those words. "We have grandparents, Andy, and this picture is of our father." She held up the picture frame for the bear to see and then laid herself back down again. "Oh, I'm so happy, Andy. They said that finding me was the greatest joy they had felt for many years. Isn't that nice? And I've so much to tell you, my dear, loyal friend, but it must wait until I have time, for today is going to be very busy indeed."

She stood the photograph back on the table and jumped out of bed, picked up Andy and then took him to the window to show him Penzance and the sea on the distant horizon. In a daze she pinched herself to make sure that she wasn't dreaming. No, she was wide awake and her future had never looked so bright.

She ate a little breakfast but was too excited to stay for long in the morning room. There was after all much to be done before she returned to London the following day and resigned from her job at the hotel. Michelle, meanwhile, insisted that Poppy again be excused from doing any of the rooms, for she knew that her daughter was eager to go out with Anna who was beginning a new chapter in her life. But before anyone went about their daily chores there were goodbyes to be said. For both Dominic and Josephina, and Meldrick and Maci were going home.

Meldrick and Maci were the first to leave and left after many hugs and kisses with those still remaining. All vowed that they must keep in touch and meet up again one day.

As they drove away, Dominic and Josephina fetched their luggage from the house and loaded it into the boot of Dominic's car.

"I...I...don't know what to say," said Anna, struggling to fight back the tears. "Were it not for you I should be going home tomorrow to a lonely bleak future. I owe you everything, Dominic, everything."

Dominic gave her a hug. "Don't be silly, Anna, that's what friends are for. Anyway, you've no idea how happy it makes me to know that I have helped you and William. Perhaps even Emily and Andy too." He took her hands in his and kissed them both. "Josephina and I really do wish you all the happiness in the world, my love."

After more hugs and kisses they too drove away. Anna waved until the car disappeared round the bend. She and Poppy then prepared to go out for the day, as planned earlier.

Anna's grandparents were already at Greenwood when Anna and Poppy arrived. Grandmother was cleaning the kitchen and Grandfather was in the back garden cutting the grass.

"I still can't believe that this was my father's house said Anna, as they all sat down in the sitting room with mugs of coffee. "I mean, it just seems so weird that I admired it the other day never dreaming that...that. Oh, I don't know what to say. Everything has changed so quickly. I feel as though my head is spinning yet at the same time I feel at peace with the world."

"Of course and we quite understand," said her grandmother, "this must all have been a great shock to you, dear. But there's no rush and you must take things at your own pace. After all, you have all the time in the world."

Grandfather smiled. "You know, William bought this house because of its name, Anna. What do you think of that?"

"Greenwood," said Anna, "he bought it because my mother's name was Greenwood?"

Grandmother nodded. "Yes, that's right. We were all house hunting at the time while in the throes of selling The Old Tile House having decided we wanted to down-size. Your grandfather and I wanted somewhere modest and William wanted somewhere to be independent." She smiled. "As soon as he saw the name on the estate agent's details he refused to look at any other houses. He made up his mind there and then that he wanted to live here even before he'd looked inside. He said it was a sign and maybe it was."

Because William Carthew had no known descendants at the time of writing his will, his home, Greenwood, was bequeathed to his parents who lived in another part of the town. However, after the discovery of the daughter William always knew that he had, his parents told Anna that the house and its contents was to be hers. This news was conveyed to Anna during her surprise visit with Poppy and Alfie the previous day. At first she had been quite bewildered and was unable to comprehend the details. But Dominic, who knew William's parents of old and had discussed it with them beforehand, explained the situation to her clearly and in great detail. When it finally sank in she was stunned.

"I found this old photo album at home this morning," said Anna's grandmother, rising and taking a book from a carrier bag. It's a few years old and most of the pictures were taken when your dad was a similar age to what you are now. I brought it along because I thought you might like to see it."

Anna eagerly took the book and looked through the pages. Several pictures were taken on the beach with St Michael's Mount in the background. Anna recognised some taken at Pentrillick. "Who are these people with my father? she asked pointing to a picture taken on the beer terrace at the Crown and Anchor. "It says summer 1988 and I've a sneaky feeling that the chap on the end is a young Dominic because his hair then is as thick as it is today."

Grandmother looked over Anna's shoulder. "Yes, you're absolutely right, it is Dominic. He and William were inseparable for many years. He even stayed with us from time to time during their school days."

"And who are the others?" Anna asked.

"The lad on the other end is Jonathan Penlow," said Grandmother, "and the girl in the middle is our dear daughter, Emily." She sighed. "So sad."

"Poor Emily," said Anna, "how cruel that she should have died so young and in such horrible circumstances too."

"Yes, her death was very tragic," said Grandfather, "We all took it badly and I don't think William was ever able to forgive himself."

"Not that it was even his fault," said Grandmother, taking a seat. "We never blamed him but it was a very distressing time, not only for us but the Penlows too. Poor Jonathan."

"Does he still live in Pentrillick?" Anna asked. "Dominic told me that he and Emily bought a cottage there."

Grandmother shook her head. "No, he left there a couple of years after Emily died. We kept in touch for a while but eventually he went up-country and married again. After that we thought perhaps it was best to let bygones be bygones."

Anna sighed. "I'm glad he was able to make a new life for himself and re-marry. I just wish you two could salvage something from your losses too."

"Oh, but we have," said Grandmother, placing her empty coffee mug on the floor, "we have you now. Our family lives on."

"Although, strictly speaking I'm not a Carthew," said Anna.

"No, but should you ever wish to change your name to Carthew then you'd have our blessing," said Grandfather, "after all, you're entitled to do so."

"Anna Emily Carthew," said Anna, dreamily. "It sounds rather nice."

"Emily," gasped Grandmother. "Your middle name is Emily?"

Anna nodded. "Yes, and I'd not made that connection till now. So do you think my mother named me that after your Emily? Oh, I do hope she did."

A broad smile crossed Grandmother's face. "I hope so too, after all they were good friends and Emily was deeply saddened when your mother left the Crown and Anchor. It left a void not only in William's life but in hers too."

Feeling uplifted, Anna turned her attention back to the photograph album and turned over the pages. When she reached the last one she gasped. For there was a picture of her parents standing hand in hand by the rose garden at The Old Tile House. The date was June 1989.

"My parents and both together, oh that's lovely." She looked up from the album. "So my mother knew The Old Tile House," she said.

Her grandmother laughed. "Oh gosh, yes. Your mother was a frequent visitor to the old house during that summer, Anna. She was fascinated by the three tall chimneys and loved its name. She loved the gardens too and used to help William with the weeding." She took in a long deep breath. "Dear William, he spent hours working on the garden and I was very sad when I found out that it was neglected after we left, but I'm told it's now back to its former glory."

"Very much so," said Poppy, "thanks to Alfie."

"And your dad," said Anna, "I believe he has worked on it too."

Poppy smiled. "Yes, between them they've done a good job."

"Was the house neglected also?" Grandfather asked. "If I remember correctly, the chap we sold it to was a plumber who in his spare time wanted to put in a lot of bathrooms so that he and his wife could eventually do bed and breakfast."

"And that's what he did," said Poppy, "put bathrooms in, I mean. Because all the bedrooms are en suite now and the house was in very good order when Mum and Dad bought it. I vaguely remember Dad saying something about the people they bought from having to sell because the wife had been offered a very good job elsewhere. Something to do with publishing, I think, and for that reason they never did do bed and breakfast."

"So, it was your parents who first ran it as a business," said Anna.

Poppy nodded. "Yes, that's right."

"And the plumber chap did everything necessary except keep the garden in order," said Grandmother, dreamily.

Poppy frowned as she thought. "Yes, well actually no. I've just remembered the conservatory. That, I believe, had to have quite extensive work done to it because the roof leaked in several places."

"Yes, I can understand that," chuckled Grandfather, "once the old vine was in leaf it took over the place - a bit like living with a triffid."

Anna felt a little light-headed on hearing mention of the vine.

"You must both come and see the place," she said, "I'm sure Michelle and James would love to see you. Don't you agree, Poppy?"

"Oh, absolutely. In fact I'll mention it to them as soon as we get back."

Anna looked again at the picture of her parents. "I know I've already said it but I really can't believe that my mother knew The Old Tile House all those years ago, and isn't it weird that I should have chosen to stay there when there were so many other places providing accommodation in Penzance."

Grandmother smiled. "But is it weird, Anna, or do you think perhaps it might have been fate?"

Anna dreamily closed the album. "I'd like to think that it was fate and that my subconscious guided me here through the love that my parents shared of this locality and The Old Tile House, but of course, we'll never know for sure."

Two weeks later, the waxing moon, almost full, beamed down on the dark sands as the evening train from London Paddington slowly rattled along the track just minutes from its destination. The passengers on the train looked from the opened windows, and watched as the waves of the ebbing tide, tumbled and splashed onto the deserted, rippled sand, before trickling back into the calm darkness of the waters beyond.

As the train slowed, Anna raised her head, put her Kindle back inside her bag, stroked Andy's furry head, and brushed cake crumbs from her lap. She then rose and reached to the rack above for her luggage containing all her worldly goods.

The train stopped and after checking that she had all her belongings, Anna walked towards the carriage door and stepped out onto the platform of Penzance station. She smiled as Alfie, and Poppy home for the weekend from university, ran down the platform to greet her. She was home.

THE END